TERMINAL VELOCITY

TERMINAL VELOCITY

A Novel
by
Dawson Vosburg

D Productions Publishing
Indiana

ISBN 978-0-615-33924-5

The names, characters, settings, events, and plot of this book are fictional or parody. Any resemblance is purely coincidental.

D Productions Publishing, an imprint of Cougar Press
1027 West 8th St.
Anderson, Indiana 46016

Printed in the United States of America
December 2009

The display text of this book is set in 14-point TS Block.
The text of this book is set in 11.5 Adobe Garamond Pro.

TABLE OF CONTENTS

For each memeber of my family:
David,
Drew,
Duncan,
Mom and Dad
(whose names are
Don and Diane).

See a pattern?

CHAPTER 1: RETURN

I think it's time to introduce you to my father.

The kitchen is an interesting place to be in my house. There's always some kind of food out on the counter that shouldn't, but other than that it's clean. The drinking water was probably the best on the block, though that's not much of a bragging point for our kitchen. It just happened to be what I thought five minutes before KC and Denise got to my house.

I, Josiah Jones, sat down at the table, left arm leaning behind my chair. This was out of habit—when I had still been in the imaginary world, I had a scar on my left arm from when my shield blew up on me. I tend to be discrete about my personal wounds, so I generally don't display them.

With my other hand I leisurely sipped my cup of water.

Dad sat at the end of the table. He tended to sit up fairly straight and peer through his glasses (which he replaced with the sleekest and slimmest style as often as possible) at his laptop, on which he worked from the tabletop.

Dad isn't very old—and Mom is even younger. They married when Dad was nineteen, Mom was eighteen, and I tripped onto the scene about two years later, preceded by my older brother, Brent.

"What's happening, Jo? I hear you have some girls coming over today," Dad said, taking his gaze off the computer for a moment.

"Yeah. No biggie."

"Neither one are dates, are they?"

"No, just friends." Perhaps I sounded agitated. I hope not.

"That's okay too. I didn't have a date till I was fifteen. Probably because I was such a nerd…" Dad smiled faintly.

"No, we just have this ongoing story that we talk about and add to every time they come over."

"Really?" Dad asked. He closed his computer and looked at me.

This was a problem. Dad rarely closed the computer and looked you straight in the eyes, but when he did, it was because of some important issue, that's for sure.

"What kind of story are you three making up?"

"Just some dumb story I've since I was young…" I said. "We just talk about our imaginary friend in this other world."

"What's in the other world?" The foreboding tone, usually accompanied by the laptop-closing and eye-looking, was mysteriously absent.

"It's just a story…a little imaginary world about secret agents and that kind of cool stuff." I hoped he wouldn't catch on somehow.

"Okay," he said. There seemed to be a tone of worry in his

voice, but he opened his computer back up.

"Dad...it's nothing—"

"I know, I know...it's just interesting, that's all."

I felt uncomfortable with the awkward pause that ensued. Dad and I were more like friends than father and son, and this conversation had been a bit...different than any other we'd had. Did he somehow know something was up with the sunglasses? Did he know that I could transport myself to another world?

These questions, however, disappeared with a knock at the door.

In a moment, we were back to the BLUE Agency.

The Top Office of the BLUE Agency surrounded us with its white walls and clean floor. I was pulled back into the world where I was a secret agent. My muscles, which had been a much smaller size in the real world, had regrown to the size that they had been during my fight against the RED Agency that had felt so far off only seconds ago.

Denise sighed. "Part one of 365," she said almost wearily.

"Why so glum about it?" I asked.

Denise shook her head and stood up, sitting at the computer on her desk. . I shrugged and glanced around for KC, but she had stealthily slipped out of the room without our notice.

Sighing deeply and beaming with a newfound excitement, I stood and strode across floor. The door opened and I was in the hallway bustling with busy agents in variations of the BLUE uniform. Most were seen in the standard BLUE wear, others sported Special- or even All-Force logos embroidered on their left and right sleeves.

I looked down at my own chest, at the BLUE logo on the left part of my shirt in light blue and white thread. I stood in this state in front of the door for a while until the rushing irritation of the people passing me became too great to ignore. I walked on.

Into my mind came the implications of this imaginary world as I stepped across the dimly lit hallways. *David and Denise, brother and sister...Steve is furious...Gary....*

I came to the most familiar of all the passages, the one that held the door for Regiment Washington in it. I stepped in front of the automatic eye, and the metal entry slid silently into the hollowed area in the wall.

Walking through the regiment, all the richness of the BLUE Agency sunk in once again. When in reality, I had lost some of the richness of this place, but my senses reminded me of my imagination's life and reality.

I thought of each agent's name as I passed the brushed metal doors. "1. 2. 3. 4..." I said to myself the numbers of the agents as I passed their room. Gary's room remained the same, and the numbers following it had not been corrected.

I stepped in the room, number 9. "Gary."

I stood for a moment, taking on all the sadness that had happened in the agent's death. I carried on, slowing my pace, and then stopping at 11. I walked inside.

David wasn't there. I looked around the room at his stuff, surprised that he wasn't in his office at this time of day. Curious, I perused his room. He was minimalist; tidy with everything he had, though it wasn't much. His desk was almost completely bare. All that sat there was a small white book, his computer's monitor, his mouse and keyboard. I leaned over to look at the curious white book. It had no title visible, plain white on all sides.

The door slid open and someone entered the room. "12?" David said.

"No, I'm 11, remember?" I said, turning to face David, who was a couple of inches taller than I was.

"Right," David said, filing the info into his brain. "What are you doing in my office?"

"Just coming over to say good afternoon."

"Okay…good afternoon, then." He quickly me to the side to sit down in the small office chair in front of his clean desk, and although the push hadn't been forceful, I struggled to keep my balance. He looked at me and shook his head.

I looked around the room. All the walls were white, all the floors blue, white, or gray. Except for the halls. The halls appeared to be made of brushed metal.

"What's that little book that you have?" I asked, pointing to the object in question.

"Um…" David said, quietly and almost musically. The word held a strange, light vibrato uncharacteristic of David. He spun and looked at the book. "It's a guidebook for government agents, a new edition. It's not out yet, but it will be tomorrow. They asked me to give the okay on it, but not to release any of the information."

"They have a guidebook for government agents?" I scratched my left arm.

"Yes, you have one in your office." David swiveled his chair around. He bore a smile, something he had had more often. Ever since he told Denise that they were twin siblings. My brain wandered to this subject for a few seconds. I knew he would be happier if he had it off his chest.

"I told you so," I said.

A confused expression replaced David's smile. "What did you tell me?"

"Oh." My brain returned to the current situation. "Never mind."

"You zoned out for a moment, Jones. But along with the book, they also have some new inventions coming out in a week or two."

"Really?"

"They're doing the wide release of the new shields...the ones that absorb energy without overloading."

It came back to my mind—the day I was with Denise in the library, the invention I had proposed.

"I actually have an invention of my own."

"Do you?" David grinned widely, revealing his meticulously cleaned teeth. "Do you have it designed, prototyped...?"

"Just an idea right now."

"Do you want to pitch it to Steve?"

My mind flew to Steve—the last time I'd seen him, we'd had an intense argument. One I shouldn't have had, one I still regret. "Steve?" I didn't mean to sound as cold as I did.

"I think he's in the invention room right now." If David noticed the tone in my voice, he didn't show it.

I glanced at a clock hanging above David's computer. "I guess I have time right now."

I strode out of the room as quickly as I could, but looking over my shoulder I saw David kept apace.

"I heard about the...argument you had with him a few weeks ago." David was as calm and collected as ever, arms swinging at his sides.

I didn't speak, instead gazing through my dark glasses at

the invention room door that was now only about ten yards away. I didn't want to talk with Steve.

"Keep it businesslike," David said. "If you don't want to talk with him, act like the argument didn't happen."

I stared at my feet. "I don't lie." I knew that this in itself was a lie…but I really didn't want to act like it never happened. *I don't really think he's unfeeling…it was a moment of anger. Couldn't Steve see that?*

David pulled the door open in a sweeping motion. "It's not a lie, it's called doing business. Business means that you don't let personal matters get in the way."

"You're just full of that, aren't you?" I said, hoping he'd react to the cold bite in my voice. To my disappointment, he merely smiled at me widely.

I shuffled inside. Steve was seated on an office chair in front of a computer, at the other end of the room. He swiveled around. "What do you two need? David? Josiah?" The tone stayed emotionless, thankfully—the last thing I wanted was to have to sound businesslike alone.

"I have an idea for an invention," I said. To my displeasure, it wasn't as businesslike in tone as I wanted it to be. "Could you have your design team on it?"

"All right—what is it you want?"

David looked at me. I sat down in another office chair beside Steve. "I need a personal transportation device. Basically, a round hoverboard with pedals that control the user's acceleration."

Steve clicked to an invention design program he had on his desktop. I looked at his setup—it had a minimalist keyboard with hexagon keys and a tablet-stylus mouse operation.

"So you want a basic hoverboard design to shift power

as you shift your weight…interesting idea…" Steve opened a terminal within the design program and typed in a code—I'm guessing it was to make a hoverboard. In a different window, a basic circular sketch was made. He tapped the center and the edge of the circle with his tablet stylus. The machinery was automatically drawn in to create the sketch completely, a perfect drawing on the screen.

"We need a place to put the foot so the person doesn't fly off," I said.

"All in good time." Steve typed more coding into the terminal, creating wiring attached to the machinery to make the electrical signals. The wiring then attached to the machinery, which in turn, would propel my invention…the one I called the Braulter. "Now we can add the feet things."

Two pedal-esque objects were added to the top and connected to the machinery. Covers for the feet were made to keep the person strapped onto the thin disk.

"Okay, generate the 3D model," David said. "Plating color: blue; material: steel; rubber type: grip. And what's the name, Josiah?"

"The Braulter."

"All right—we'll call it the B series then for 'Braulter,'" Steve said.

Steve typed in the information and a new window appeared in the program. A black background was there, and a blue metal object sat in the center of the view. Steve rotated the virtual camera around the virtual object to show off all of its aspects.

"I'll have the rest of the building team look over it and we'll have a beta made in a couple of weeks. I'll mark on the calendar that the presentation is to be two weeks from tomorrow. Too bad I won't be around for it."

"What do you mean?" I asked. "Why not?"

I scratched my left arm, where a ragged scar had been left after my shield blew during the invasion of the RED Agency. Frederick had hit me too many times and blew my shield, followed by a pistol whip to the head. Fortunately, the blow had missed its intended mark of my temple, creating less of an impact than Frederick, the evil commander of the RED, had desired.

"The autopsy. It starts the same day as the presentation day—three weeks from tomorrow."

"Why didn't you choose another date then?"

A chilling expression was pinned to his face. "This is the only open slot."

I stared at the computer screen, the 3-D model of my invention. I didn't want it anymore. It wasn't worth this.

He stood and began to walk away.

The cold expression on his face remained as he walked out of the room. David and I looked at each other. I shook my head. He was still angry at me about the day in the medical bay—the day he and I had fought about whether or not he really felt bad at all for Gary. I had acted explosively when I found they were doing an autopsy. It felt dishonoring, a lessening of Gary. He wasn't a cat in a biology class.

"What happened to businesslike?" David said.

I stood up as well, slowly taking footsteps to the door, not listening to a word David said.

CHAPTER 2: A PRESENTATION TO REMEMBER

The workout gym was full of conversation. Tom, Bob, David, Denise—everyone in my inner circle was there except KC. KC had been mysteriously absent for the past couple of weeks, ever since we'd gotten back. She said she was working on something and hadn't said what…but I had other things on my mind.

As the talk flew around me, peppered with the occasional laugh, I was recalling going to my office after my failed attempt at businesslike.

I had sat at my computer, slamming the keys on the keyboard as I typed in my password. I checked my e-mail, angered that there were no new messages.

I stood, and in a moment of rage, thrust my chair as hard as I could across the room, causing it to hurtle into my nightstand and into the wall with a pair of loud bangs.

I ran to the scene of the wrecked nightstand, feeling embarrassed for this act of stupidity. Everything looked fine—my alarm clock was sturdy, and the nightstand itself was made of metal. Underneath was my e-journal.

I picked it up. I had forgotten about it for quite a while now. I had to write something in it.

Hastily I put the nightstand back up and replaced the clock and books on top of it. In my journal, I wrote:

Steve…why does he have to hold a grudge like this? And why is the only emotion I see come from him anger towards me? It's completely unfair not only to me, but to other people.

I wonder if he just has a problem with interaction, because that's all I've seen. But still…I can't just fume about it all day. All I can do now is avoid talking to him as much as I can.

I put down the e-j. My mind felt calmer now. *I can't talk to Steve. That will only make things worse. I just have to leave it to cool.…*

A beep issued from my personal communicator, my percom. I picked up the silver-blue cell and checked the caller ID.

It was someone I had never heard of—Lewis Trenton. Should I pick it up?

It beeped again, then a second later, again. I made up my mind—I pressed talk.

"Who is this?" I said in a kind tone, trying to hide any evidence of what I'd been thinking of.

"You're late, Jones."

The voice was snappy, cold, and hard-edged.

"Who is this?" I struggled to stay calm.

"Lewis Trenton."

"I know that." I was losing patience, and it was unfortunately evident in my tone.

"Of course you do. Denise probably told you about me…"

"Who are you?"

"Regiment Aerei. Agent 4. Section 3. But that's just a job description."

"And what am I late for?"

"The negotiations have been delayed long enough. But perhaps you haven't received your invitation yet?"

"Listen, I don't know what these negotiations are. And there's no such thing as Regiment Aerei. If this is a stupid prank, then—"

"There's no such thing in your agency as Regiment Aerei." His voice was becoming annoyingly calm.

"Who are you kidding?" I became instantly wary. This guy was a RED agent. Why was I even talking to him?

"Oh yes, right…I believe you haven't received your invitation yet. I think they'll be sending it to you whenever it is most convenient."

"Now wait a minute—"

The line went dead. All I heard was a long *beeeeep* . Frustrated once again, I jabbed the personal communicator back on my belt.

I remembered all these things at the strangest time, running on the treadmill. Who was Lewis Trenton? What did "negotiations" mean?

Then, suddenly, I remembered that I was holding the treadmill, my mouth hanging open, and my pace slow. I upped it a few miles per hour to four. I noticed that no one was talking anymore. I struck up a conversation. Now's not the time to think about that.

"David, how did the guidebook go? I was looking it over today, and found some pretty useful tips."

"You used to know almost every detail in that book before, and you just lost it in what seemed to be minutes," David answered. He remembered the first time I had entered the BLUE Agency for real. Did he know?

I cringed inside. *I have to get off this subject, just say something that'll end the conversation.* "I never quite understood why," I lied. "I can remember having all of my training, then the memories are fuzzy…"

I sighed and continued plodding along. Turned up the speed to 4.7.

"If you've gotten over most of that 'fuzziness,' then why do you think any of the stuff in that book is new or helpful?" Bob asked as he jogged at five miles per hour.

"Don't waste your breath," David said with a laugh. "There were quite a few new features to the book—I was one of the editors. Then again it was tiresomely standard-issue."

"And I hear that the new and improved shields are going to be released soon," Tom said. "I'm pretty excited about that. And I hear they've got are a ton of new features."

"What kind of 'new features' could there be?" Denise asked.

"The ones that don't burn out," Bob said. "I was excited about that, mostly."

Denise laughed. "I've had those for half a year. Guess you guys are unlucky. I hear it's only going to be a limited release. In fact, I signed a paper saying it was." I heard in her voice her hatred toward paperwork.

"They're currently just manufacturing enough to go

'round to the higher ranking agents," David said, "but by the time they're done streamlining production the process will be cheap enough to make it standard issue."

Denise dismounted the stationary bike and stepped onto one of the treadmills. She pushed the buttons to a slow, comfortable starting pace. "Speaking of new inventions, Josiah: when is the prototype 1 presentation of your Braulter happening?"

My eyes widened. "That's tomorrow! I had completely forgotten." Lewis Trenton had overtaken so much of my mind for the past two weeks.

Tom shook his head.

I pushed my pace to 6 mph, a minute later, 7, and up one every time until I reached 10, where I ran steadily. The conversation was replaced with harsh exercise and thought. I had to tell Denise about the message. She needed to know.

After almost an hour on the machine, I turned to cool down. The speed decreased rapidly, and soon I was going at only one mile per hour. My breathing was quick and shallow. "Thousand and a quarter calories burned," I said. I felt my tired leg muscles, still tensed but weakened from the strain.

I turned off the machine, wiped the perspiration from the handles, and stepped off. Denise had already started to walk out; the others were finishing their runs on the machines.

I caught up with Denise. "Good workout today, eh, Josiah?" she said.

"Listen, I need to cut to the chase with you right now," I said with intensity in my voice.

Denise perked up. "Who contacted you?"

I stopped, taken aback. "How did you know what I was going to say?"

"Nothing...I mean, I didn't...carry on." She resumed her usual state.

I mentally logged her little slip of information. "I received a call on my personal communicator from Lewis Trenton, someone whom I believe to be an agent from the RED Agency." I started to walk again, stepping into the stairwell and walking up.

"Hmm," Denise said slowly in a suddenly airy tone. "Yes, he is a RED agent. That's odd. Thank you for the information, Josiah." She sprinted up the steps and vanished into the next-to-lowest floor. I heard her talking with David...I could almost hear David smiling.

"That was odd." I walked up the stairs to the Regiment Washington headquarters, no wiser about Lewis Trenton than when I'd started working out.

Presentation day.

I was dressed in clean clothes, loosely fitting, and the usual light t-shirt with the BLUE logo embroidered on the left breast pocket. Dark jeans, boot cut, 32-30 size. Everything ironed and crisp.

A beep gave me a start. I stared at my belt, eyebrows raised at the percom. What does he want?

After hearing it beep four times, I finally picked it up. "Listen, I know you're a RED agent. And an old friend of Denise's, I perceive. I don't want any of this crap about negotiations or whatever—"

"I need you to send Denise a message." Trenton remained calm.

The interruption left me speechless for a few seconds, gaze stuck to the white wall of the other end of the room.

"Oh…so you want to deliver a message from her old RED Agency buddy?"

"Josiah, don't be—"

"Since when are we on a first name basis? If you have a message for her, deliver it yourself." I retained a defiant composure to my speech.

I mashed the disconnect button as hard as I could. In my rational brain I knew that I shouldn't have done that—should have tried to find out who he was indirectly—but I didn't want to right now. I instead stalked toward my nightstand, intending to write my seething feelings into my e-j.

I remembered the task at hand and checked the clock before I could reach the stand. The presentation was supposed to have started five minutes ago.

"Dang it," I said to myself, standing and hurtling to the door. It slid open before I reached it as Denise walked into the room.

"You're late. Where have you been?" she said.

"Just received an unimportant message, a nuisance."

Denise nodded, and I walked out of the room behind her.

In the invention room, chairs were aligned in an arc so people could watch the presentation comfortably. I stood on the left of the invention's stand, opposite one of the main inventors in the BLUE Agency, Harold Ferdinand.

The chairs were already filled—mostly restless agents from the Washington regiment, but also several from other regiments and Denise, who took her seat next to David and whispered to him. He nodded.

Harold, the agent heading the Invention department,

smiled and moved behind the pedestal that held Prototype-1 of the Braulter, which was going to be formally called the B5.

Each person watched intently now. An impatient look was on every face.

Clearing his throat, Harold said, "Josiah Jones, Agent 11 of Regiment Washington, it is my honor to present to you Prototype-1 of the B5." He pulled the green cloth sheet off of the invention.

A sleek, blue steel covering hid the intricate machinery of the compact circular device. Two footpedals sat on top in the center, between which were three buttons extruding from the surface. "B5" was printed on the very front of the Braulter.

"The top inventors have modified your original design, making small tweaks and improvements. For instance, we have added three kick buttons onto the front interface, allowing you to shift the status from ON/OFF for the right button, STANDBY for the center, and AUTO-CRUISE for the left. Auto-Cruise takes you at an even pace of 17 miles per hour, and it stays consistent no matter how hard you lean forward."

I nodded, impressed. *They thought up every thing I didn't.* "May I?" I moved my hand to touch the B5.

"Sure, go ahead," said Harold.

I lifted the B5 and placed it gently on the ground, slid my left foot in the pedal, and gently depressed the ON/OFF button with my right before quickly putting my foot in the opposite pedal.

I was lifted almost a foot from the floor. Smoothly, the Braulter moved forward in a small circle, turning at my direction. It was like being weightless yet on a solid surface.

I pushed the ON/OFF button once again, and with grace I was lowered to the gray-carpeted floor.

Dismount was easy, more so than I anticipated.

"Also, as you may have seen or felt, the pedals conform around your feet for security and comfort." Harold smiled. The invention team made *genius* stuff.

I lifted the B5 back onto the pedestal. "Thank you, Harold. I can speak for everyone in this room when I say that I will be looking forward to the final release of the B5."

Bang.

The door slammed against the wall. The handle must have made an indent.

A huffing man burst inside the room, panting. Steve's small glasses flew across the room. "Josiah!"

I stepped toward Steve. Reflexively, my right hand gripped my pistol. "What code are we in?"

"Not danger, Josiah, but it will cause some," Steve said between breaths. He fixed the position of his glasses with a glance.

"Then—"

I had no time to finish my sentence before Steve shouted, "Josiah, Gary's not dead!"

The words hit me like a bullet to the chest. I leaped into the air with surprise and shock.

Steve still breathed in and out quickly. Rubbing his eyes, he bounded across the room and put his wiry glasses back on.

"He's not dead! The body we found was a fake! A model! And well done, might I say. The RED Agency did a very good job of—"

"Stop...we can't discern whether or not he's dead. He could be in the RED Agency right now." I tried and failed to calm myself...the words came out in a disorganized, sputtering rush. "What was it if it wasn't Gary?"

I caught a glimpse of Tom, sorry I had had that argument. Another thing I'd messed up with my lack of control. I gave him an apologetic look—he nodded, as if he'd understood.

"It was a model. Very well constructed, no doubt artificial skin. They have materials that look and feel real. Just add to that a pale, dead-looking color and laser-map Gary's face and features into it, and you have a convincing mock-up that would work just fine for faking a death," Steve said, his voice sharp and quick.

I came close to falling on the floor there, in front of most of the regiment. *Tom was right the whole time.*

My stomach sank, my muscles twitched. My knowledge of the imaginary world and the events current with it were crashing down, and I didn't know whether to be happy, sad, or outraged.

CHAPTER 3: TOM, THEORIST

Left with nothing to say, I ran out of the room, tripping over my own feet and collapsing on myself as I fell in my office. My arms felt raw with rug burn.

I picked up my e-j and stylus, and wrote:

What am I going to do about Gary? Someone has to find where he is…I know he's in the RED Agency base somewhere. He has to be….

All these things are piling on top of each other. Now I've got to make amends with Tom and Steve and I still don't know what the heck is going on with this Trenton guy. Maybe I need to call him back—I don't know. And now this of all things?

I stared at the screen of my e-j, reading the words over and over again. I unhooked my personal communicator, opened my recent calls section, and called Lewis Trenton. *I can't believe I'm doing this.*

"So," said the biting voice on the other end, "*you're* calling *me* now, eh?"

"Yes, Trenton, regrettably, I am calling you. I just need to ask you a few questions."

"And what would these questions be, Jones?"

I felt a bit of thankfulness that he decided not to call me Josiah, for him not to soil that name, and this helped quell my anger. "Are you an agent for the crime syndicate RED?" I asked slowly, as if I was asking him about the weather.

"You could say that," said Trenton. I could tell by the sound of his voice that he had a sinister smile on his face.

"All right. Now, were you, or are you, an associate of Denise Black?"

He chuckled. "I used to be…you might say that I still am."

"Okay…now, what are these delegations you're babble—uh, that is to say, talking—about?" I swallowed, my throat constricted. The words weren't coming out as I meant.

"You'll find out…hmm, probably tomorrow night."

"What—"

But the conversation was over. He had hung up on me, and once again I was left disappointed. *But at least I have some information—and Denise might have some explaining to do.*

My room echoed with the sound of paces, steps echoing across the wide white walls, my thoughts bouncing inside my head.

Tired, I sat in my office swivel chair. How? Why? I don't understand why they would choose Gary to steal and…fake his death….

The door slid open fast. Quick steps followed. Tom approached. I turned around to see his dodgy expression, smirking at me like a car salesman.

"I was right," Tom said.

I leaned far back in my chair, far as its thick frame would go back.

"I know you were," I said, hushed and tense. "But why did they choose him? Why Gary? Why not me?"

"Because you were too important," Tom said. "I already explained this before."

"That was when you had no evidence," I snapped.

"I did have evidence."

"That was when I didn't know!" My voice had risen to its limits with anger and frustration. The moment was so gloriously angry. The tones rang aloud across the room, echoing seconds after the words had been said, and the anger faded. "I don't remember your entire theory. Explain it, would you?"

Tom, still smiling, said, "Do you mind if I pull up a chair?"

He gestured to a more comfortable white lounge chair that I had sitting next to my computer. No one had ever used it.

"Uh...sure," I said, letting the pause hang for a few seconds.

Tom dragged the chair next to me. I swiveled around, played with the height adjustment, and looked at Tom and waited for his explanation to begin.

"Gary seemed to be a pretty inconsequential character in this little game here. Sure, he might have been a top agent, and he was in All-Force, but it's not a big deal, right? He didn't necessarily have any information." Tom looked at me like he was expecting an answer.

"Um…well, come to think of it, he was in the All-Force 5."

"It was a rhetorical question. The answer, if I were asking for one, would be that he was on the mission with you. None of the other facts are important. But why would this seem important? We really didn't have many secret plans. There wasn't much he could have known. Right?" Tom paused. I felt uncomfortable. "Wrong again."

"Huh?"

"I did a little digging on this. Meaning I asked him if he had read Denise's tell-all RED Agency book. He *had* read it, even though only you, Bob and David read it that you know about. So he knew all the secrets. But in reality, that doesn't matter, because they thought all of us had read the book."

"How would they know we had the book?"

"How else would we know where their headquarters was? And besides, wouldn't that be something they would like to find out themselves? So, they planned this ahead a bit, had a model made, and planted it in the second battle in our own home base, which was merely a cover-up chance to capture Gary."

My mind digested the information. All the pieces fit together now. He had made some sense out of it.

"Any more questions?" Tom lengthened his words.

"No." I leaned forward. "Tom, listen…I'm sorry for being so condescending to you when I thought Gary was dead. I just…I thought you were being disrespectful, that's all. But now—"

He grabbed my hand and shook it quickly. "Hey, don't sweat it. We've got other things to worry about." He looked like he was coming up with another plan.

"I see that in your eyes. What are you thinking?"

Tom leaned forward and whispered so no one else could possibly hear. "I have a feeling that the BLUE is going to take too long to get into this case here—we need to take some action of our own before the RED dispose of their little prisoner."

"Action?" I said. His words piqued my interest.

"We need to take matters into our own hands if we're going to be able to get Gary rescued in time. They're going to bleed every word from his mouth before the BLUE can send in an investigator to find out squat. I've got some ideas of my own." Tom smiled and rubbed his hands together, slowly and silently.

I stood up abruptly. "No, no, no. None of your crazy conspiracy plans. Granted, you were right this one time, but that still doesn't justify you trying to drag—"

"Don't think of it that way," Tom said. "Sure, I made a few little theories in the past, but this isn't one of those times. I'm just showing you the cold hard facts about what is going to happen. The BLUE will send in an investigator to look things over, think about what happened, and then they'll send in a search commission three months later! We can't let that happen."

I shook my head back and forth, as if I were a dog expelling water from its fur. "No! You don't understand, Tom. We work for the BLUE. I would probably be that investigator."

"But we could be back here with Gary in less time than it would take for them to send us in. Admit it, 12. This is the fastest way we're ever going to see Gary again." Tom's words came straight and clear.

I sighed deep and long, expelling every bit of air in my

lungs. I sat in the chair and leaned back. Forward. Back again. I looked into Tom's face.

"Are you coming with me, Jo?"

A minute of silence followed. "Yes." I made sure the word rang loud and clear.

Tom extended his hand, clutched mine with a sturdy grip and hearty shake. A smile broke on his face, and I couldn't help but share the expression.

The next day, I was in Tom's office in the PRLO section of the main HQ. We had it all figured out.

"We leave tonight," Tom proposed.

"Tonight? Why so soon?" I said. "Don't we need a little more time to plan this than just *today?*"

"What's there to plan? Besides, this is an emergency mission. All we need to plan is getting out of here tonight without being seen." He looked up at the ceiling in thought, hand on his chin, which was rough with stubble. He had grown older, gotten taller, looked more mature than when I had first met him at his own main base in Pennsylvania.

"What are you thinking about? It isn't hard to get past the night guard if you're an agent. And since I'm the top agent besides Denise, I already have automatic clearance."

"But they'll wonder why we're carrying a bunch of equipment and other stuff in suitcases. How are we going to hide that?" Tom rubbed his forehead.

I thought for a moment. "We could go out the backdoor—it's the entrance to the parking garage, door 4E. That one's not very heavily guarded—only one guy ever stays posted there."

"But that's still one guy. How can we get past him?"

"At the changing of the guard. Every two hours, starting at eight, there's a changing between the three night guards who guard that door. One happens to be at two o'clock in the morning, which is an hour or two after everyone's asleep."

"Now you're thinking!" A bright smile once again cracked Tom's face.

I smiled back at him. "What do we need to bring that'll be so big or cumbersome that people would wonder why we're bringing it?"

"The B5."

I froze. An awkward silence overtook the place, giving it an eerie feel. "What?"

"We need to take the prototype B5."

"Why? That's taking it way too far," I said. Always have to have something to—

"It's the perfect infiltrator device," replied Tom. "It'll be able to get us into the RED base, wherever their new one is."

"How can you be sure it'll be able to infiltrate anything? You don't really know much about—"

"Yes, I do. I thought about this all at the time when the presentation was going on. I knew we could use it for this."

I pounded my fist on my leg. "Dang it, Tom! Why do you always plan out these impossible ideas? And why were you thinking about getting Gary before it was confirmed that he was still alive? And above all, they've never tested to see if the B5 will be able to stand up in battle."

"I think it will. The B5 is fast enough to outrun any person on foot, and quiet enough to slip through a hall almost silently. Also, there are no handles, so you can attack at the same time as you float down the hall. Put a silencer on the gun, and you're golden."

Dang it, he's right again, I thought. I leaned back again in the identical twin to the white lounge chair that also sat next to Tom's computer desk. "Okay, I'm still with you. And a couple of the new shields that were just released, right?" I said.

"Yeah, I was actually given mine yesterday," Tom said. "Heh. Convenient."

CHAPTER 4: SNEAKING OFF

Night approached quickly. I barely had time to do any of my packing for the dangerous, outrageous and strangely exciting mission with Tom. Why do I trust him again?

I shirked off the feelings of doubt and continued packing. I put it into my mind that this was just like a real mission, just as mandatory.

I put my last article of clothing into my small white suitcase. Placed it under my bed. Sat at my computer.

The door slithered open. I turned my seat around. David strode in.

"You didn't come to talk yesterday, after what happened at the presentation," he said. "Denise said she'd had to pick you up from your office beforehand, and then you don't even stay to talk after the meeting."

I squirmed uncomfortably in my seat.

"What is it, Josiah?"

"I was with Tom. We were talking about…Gary." I shuffled again.

"Of course you were. What else would you be talking about yesterday? Otherwise it was fairly uneventful." A smile spread across David's face, carrying little emotion. The expression quickly faded.

He doesn't know about my conversation with Trenton. That's something to talk about. I realized that I still hadn't told Denise about that. I skipped over the subject in my mind.

"The B5 was smooth. It ran excellently."

"I see," David answered. "What do you think BLUE is going to do about Gary? I suspect they would send in an investigator to find RED's latest HQ."

My efforts were turned down. "It'll take them a while to do that," I said. I chuckled halfheartedly. "Don't you think?"

"Considering the urgency of this and his deep involvement in the mission, it may be less than a week before they send someone to the base. That is, once they find it." David scratched at his buzzed hair. "They'll probably be able to get someone to the RED base before Gary says anything. Do you doubt his resilience?" David asked.

I felt pressured. "No…er…that's a tough question. I don't doubt that he's a good guy and won't willingly break, but the RED can be ruthless. If it takes us a week, who knows what could happen?"

"He'll know that he has to buy us some time." David removed his sunglasses, cleaned them with his shirt, and placed them back on. "He's known that for a while."

"Let's hope so," I said. *I can't believe we're really being so composed. It's Gary we're talking about! But I guess that's just*

David, isn't it?

"I should be going. I have to do a workout today. I haven't had one since day before yesterday. I need my exercise."

David's parting words seemed strangely like a riddle. I shook my head as the door slithered open then shut as David left the room.

He suspects something, I know it. Quickly I abandoned the idea and turned to my computer.

One o'clock approached quickly, as I headed to the PRLO section of the BLUE headquarters. Into Tom's office. Tom turned around in his office chair to face me.

"Good, you're here! That's great. It's almost one o'clock. We need to get ready, fast. Do you have yourself packed?"

"Yep." I sat in a white lounge chair.

"Good. I packed mine last night before I went to bed so no one watched me." Tom rested his hands behind his head and smiled, perhaps out of nervousness.

"Good idea—I packed after lunch today, and was lucky not to get caught by David. So, when are we getting the B5?" I scratched my scarred arm nervously.

"Right now would be good." Tom stood. "Do you want to get it, or do you want me to?"

"I'd better go get it." I began to walk leisurely to the brushed steel door.

"Okay." Tom sat back in his office chair. "Be in your office as soon as you have it. I'll come there to meet you with my stuff."

"How are you going to sneak that past everyone without getting noticed?" I stopped at the doorway, just far enough so the automatic sliding door wouldn't slip into the wall.

"I put it in my duffel bag I usually use for the gym. I'll say that I'm going to put it in for a workout tomorrow morning if anyone gets suspicious, which they shouldn't."

"Why?" I asked.

"Because they *should* be in bed."

I shook my head and walked through the door. I tried not to make any noise as my feet touched the ground, using tactics I had been taught in my training.

I thought to myself as I walked through the base, through to the Washington regiment headquarters. *This is probably going to end up being worth it. I'm going to think, "Why did I ever doubt Tom?"*

The invention room in the Washington section was before me. I opened the manual door. To my relief, it was unlocked. I stepped into the room with great caution.

Steve was on the other side. He heard me enter. "Hey, Josiah. What do you need?" His voice sounded friendly.

"Um...I need to borrow the B5 for a couple days, test out how it works. Would that be okay?" I crossed my fingers. I don't think he saw it.

"Sure, 12. You can borrow it for a while. It's not too important." Steve returned to his work.

"Thanks," I said. He had remembered that I was 12 again. Another pang of guilt shot through me.

"Mmhmm," Steve said without looking up from his work.

I picked up the B5, and looked toward the door. I thought again. *I need to fix something before I go.* I placed the B5 back on the pedestal and walked to Steve's computer.

"Is there something else you need?"

"Listen...about what happened in my hospital room. I..." I tried to think of the words I meant. "I was being insensitive. It had nothing to do with you. I get where you were coming from."

Steve smiled. "Thanks, Josiah."

I stepped back and frowned. "What'd I do?"

"Apologized. I wanted to…to forgive you, but it really… never mind. You can go back to what you were doing."

He sat back on his computer and began typing again. Picking up the B5, I strode out of the room with a spring in my step, relief and excitement washing over me.

Tom was already waiting for me when I entered my room.

"Hey, Josiah. I found your suitcase under the bed. That thing is small enough to fit in my bag!" he said. He opened his bag and showed me the small suitcase.

"I don't over-pack. Besides, it shouldn't be too much of a stretch to stop at a Laundromat."

Tom chuckled. "We'll see."

The changing of the guard happened in two minutes.

Tom and I crouched in a narrow and nearly unused hallway that turned into Entrance E4. The guard would wake up the next guard adjacent to the door out, and we would have thirty seconds to get through the door and in the garage.

I carried Tom's weighty bag, which contained everything we brought.

"Do you think the other guard will see us, walking into position?" Tom mouthed to me. Agents were trained in reading lips, which I often found to come in handy.

"Probably not. If he does, he won't think much of it."

The guard stepped away from the door and down another

hallway to inform the other guard, who was currently asleep, that it was his shift.

A thrill, a rush of adrenaline pumped in me as I stood and silently ran for the door. With a great heave, Tom pulled it open. I jumped into the garage and Tom closed the door behind him, just as the guard awakened and walked to his post.

My breathing was quick and heavy. The sound of the guard's footsteps as he took his place at the door seemed very loud.

"That was a close one," I said quietly.

"Not really," Tom said as he began to walk toward his car. "I've been in closer scrapes before. That was nothing."

I rolled my eyes. "Why am I not surprised?"

I tossed the bag in the back of the car carefully, closed the trunk, and sat down in shotgun.

Tom put the key in the ignition. The car fired up immediately.

Excitement welled in my stomach as the engine revved and the car pulled out of the parking space.

The car sped out of the base and into the large field outside. It ran onto the small country road off to the interstate.

"What's our first destination?"

"Somewhere to find our answer to where the base is. Their new setup has to be somewhere, and I'm not guessing it would be a small rural town." His intense expression could be seen in the darkness.

"Why not?" I looked at him, puzzled.

"You've met Frederick, right?"

"Yeah."

"And you've seen his top office, right?"

"Mmhmm."

"Does he seem to be one that would like to settle his base in some country farm area? No, he'll have it near some big city."

"Why?" I asked.

"He can blend in. Not him as a person—I mean that the higher levels of technology can blend in with higher tech surroundings. That's probably why their bases are in bigger cities and towns than BLUE bases."

"Where do you think this could be, though? Chicago?" I asked. "That's a place full of crime, I know that."

"Eh, I don't know about Chicago. Too obvious." He looked out his window, at the wide road he drove on. "We're going to need to do some research."

I thought a moment. "Bryan McQueen's basically the BLUE's guru. We could check into New York."

"Why would we want to do that? He's another BLUE agent. He would probably turn us in and say we were rogue or something." Tom directed his stare back through the windshield. "No, we can't go with Bryan."

"I beg to differ. Perhaps we could convince him to join us…"

"Yeah, sure, that's real likely, Josiah."

"I don't know. He just has something in him. That right spirit that I'm looking for in a person to join us."

"What put the idea in your head that we wanted more people here?" Tom looked at me incredulously. "We're not going to do that. I'm sorry, but we can't afford to get caught. I'm the one who's driving."

"That can be changed." I looked at Tom with a deathly gaze.

Tom rolled his bright brown eyes. "Don't threaten me.

It won't do you any good. Besides, if you try to hijack this car you'll be in more trouble."

I sighed.

"Are we still going to New York? Or where were you thinking for the research part of our trip?"

"Library of Congress, maybe…it helped you guys the last time you went on a mission like this. Do you have a laptop with you?"

"No."

"Dang it." He slammed his hand on the wheel. "We'll have to share mine. We can go and get that book…"

"Denise's book?" The car was quiet for a minute. Tom's hands were clenched around the steering wheel. Knuckles white, veins visible through his skin. "What's wrong?"

"Yes, Denise's book."

"Why are you so angry all of a sudden?" I asked.

"It just makes me angry, that's all." The car went around a long, wide turn.

"Why is that?"

"Don't get all psychological on me. It just gets me fired up whenever I hear about what she did. She was evil, Jo. Do you mind if I call you Jo?"

"But she's not evil anymore."

Tom sighed. A deep sigh, filled with a variety of emotions, I could tell.

The car continued rolling down the smooth road. North.

Many hours passed. The Dodge Charger had comfortable seats, a radio, and a CD player—yet we played no music. It seemed that Tom had wanted complete silence, so I stayed quiet even though I wanted music to help relax me a bit and drown out the sound of the wheels spinning, the engine running the car in constant motion.

I gathered my thoughts and said, "Tom, can we turn on some music?"

He wordlessly handed me a case of CDs. I began flipping through—some bands I hadn't heard of, some I had but didn't like. Then I came to an audiobook. It was a Charles Dickens novel, but the title was almost completely scratched out.

Disc 4 of 10, it said. Next to it was the letter *G,* but this was written in Sharpie. Thin, green Sharpie.

"Tom, what's this?" I asked. "The title is scratched out, and there's a G written on it."

Tom looked at the disc. "Where did that come from?" he mumbled. He took the disc out of the case and put it in the slot of the player.

Following a few minutes of silence, the sound came. "If you are hearing this CD, then you must be Tom and Josiah, Agent 15 of PRLO and Agent 12 of WTN. We know who you are." The voice issued with a heavy French accent and a dark, deep tone.

Tom and I looked at each other with fear.

"Don't panic." The voice was firm. "You will not find the information you need in the Library of Congress, as you thought. The same book you read won't be able to work. That doesn't have the correct information."

I stared at the CD player, mouth wide open. No words could say what shock I felt.

"Listen closely to what I say and make sure you write it down. This recording is an extra layer added onto the original CD and is being burned off as it plays, so you will only hear this once. I will give you thirty seconds to grab a pad of paper and a writing utensil."

Pushing aside inconsequential objects with my hands, I looked around and saw a hotel pad of paper and pen. I picked them up quickly and waited the remaining 22 seconds.

"Go to the website URL https://gr.bl.re/R1654/b3.htm. There you will find information on where you are to find the information you need. I will leave the rest to the website to disclose," said the messenger.

My fingers flew as they scribbled the URL for the website.

"I'll tell you the website once again: https://gr.bl.re/ R1654/b3.html."

I finished writing the website out and put the notebook down.

"One final thing—when you arrive at your final destination, you will meet a planted representative from our organization. We need to discuss several things with your own agency. Thank you. JCDO."

"JCDO?" I said, confused. "What does that stand for?"

"I don't know, but we have to look at that web address. We're at an exit right now. I'm pulling over and we're going to a gas station. I'll go in to keep them from thinking we're loitering, and you stay here and look at that web address." Tom turned the wheel and the car spun through the exit to the gas stop.

"But how do you know this isn't some trick?" I said. "There must be some sort of virus or something on that site."

"Don't be ridiculous," Tom said. "Whatever is on that website, this computer can handle."

I nodded in admittance.

The brakes ended the car's journey through the wide road that we had traveled on for a few hours. We were now in southern New York, an hour or two from the city.

"I'm going in," Tom said. He stepped out of the car and went into the gas station, where he waited outside the bathroom.

I picked up his computer, which was resting in a black bag between the two seats. I opened it up, turned it on, and opened the web browser. I typed in the web address, copying from the sloppily-written URL on my little hotel notepad. The website was long in coming up, even for this fast of a computer. The page finally showed. There were three colored bars at the top of the screen. One was for red, one was for green, and one was for blue. The RED bar was automatically selected for me, and the page was strangely scrolled down without my interference.

Several pictures of a skyscraper appeared on the screen, as well as scans from the original blueprint, videos of the offices, and pictures of nearly every room inside. Across the top was written "*LOCATION: New York, NY.*"

My eyes widened. We were an hour and a half away from the RED base. And it was above ground.

Another line of text: "*How to infiltrate: This one is tricky. It looks as if it were a regular business office building. If you look through the windows, you will see people working like regular office workers, unless it is night. It's in the middle of the building where your troubles come in.*"

I frowned as I read.

"*This is where all of the agents are bunked, where the holding cells are, etcetera, etcetera. This is what the real base part of it is. Although the entire thing is owned by the RED, the inside part is the place you will probably be going to infiltrating. This is almost impossible to do because the offices on the outside of the building look like normal offices, and you will look like a criminal with high technology. You want to infiltrate the center directly, but this is difficult to do since the roof is shaped like a pyramid."*

I shook my head slowly.

"The way you get past this? You need to find a way to land on the very top of the building. There is an upper room that is at the very top below the roof that serves only as a place where on occasion, Frederick himself will come to contemplate his missions and ideas.

"At the top of the building is a four-foot-wide square section of the roof, and then a three-foot section of glass. You can use glass cutting machinery to enter the upper room, and if you are lucky, Frederick won't be there to intercept you."

I looked at the screen, baffled. How were we going to land at the top of the building on a four-foot space? Both of us?

I looked at Tom, who had gotten out of the bathroom long ago and had been browsing the store for more things to buy. He motioned for me to come in the store.

I folded the computer and got out of the car and through the sliding glass doors. I walked into the candy aisle, where Tom looked hungrily at the sweets.

"We don't have enough money to buy that," I said. I thought about what had just come out of my mouth. "Wait a minute—we don't have any money!"

"You speak too soon." Tom put his hands into his back pocket, into his wallet, and then to the cash fold. Ten one-hundred-dollar bills sat inside.

"Where did you get that?" I said.

"It was from my most recent payment." A smirk grew

across Tom's face.

I shook my head. "We would have fairly unlimited money if we had the BLUE backing us," I said. "Man, why couldn't we wait for them to get us before we took stupid action on it?"

"It isn't stupid, and we couldn't wait. We had no choice. We can get past the RED if we just try. Play along and watch what happens." Tom picked up six packages of gummy worms and walked to the faux-marble counter. Behind it stood a bewildered teenager watching our conversation with a strange face. You couldn't blame her—she had little else to do.

I followed him as he carelessly tossed the bags of candy onto the counter. They scattered across it and nearly fell to the ground. The young employee stopped them from falling. She scanned one of them six times with the laser, adding up the costs on the computer. "Ten forty-five," she said weakly.

Tom opened up his wallet and put a Benjamin on the counter. "It's the smallest one I've got."

The girl's eyelids, thick with makeup, opened wide. "Okay," she said, unable to say anything else.

The computer added up the amount of change and dispensed the coins, which Tom dropped in the "take a penny, leave a penny" bin. The cashier counted four twenties, one five and four ones and handed them to Tom quietly.

"Thanks."

The girl slowly piled the candy into a bag, one by one, and handed them to Tom. He stuffed his change into his wallet and led me back into the car. I followed awkwardly.

Tom leaped into the car at an alarming pace and started it up before I could open the door. I looked at him and shook my head.

"Where is the new base?" Tom talked as if nothing had happened.

"New York City," I said, clipping my seat belt across my chest. "I was right."

The car pulled away from the store's parking lot. "Convenient. Where in NYC? Outside of it and underground, or is it a small building?"

"It's a skyscraper." I opened up the laptop to prove it to him. He looked at the text, the pictures—everything. There was even an address below the photographs.

"Get into MapQuest. We need to find out how we get to this thing."

"Hold your horses, buddy!" I said, slamming down my armrest. "We're going to need a plane to get onto this one."

"Impossible! We're talking about a 4-foot space here. All we need is a strong grappling hook gun."

"Then we'll just look like robbers." I looked at Tom as we sped down the highway.

"Hmm," Tom said thoughtfully. "Where could we get a jet?"

"Tom!"

"Hmm?"

"Bryan McQueen!"

CHAPTER 5: BRYAN MCQUEEN

"What?" Tom said. "We already had this discussion. No one is coming with us."

"We need him this time. There's no way we're going to get a plane to drop us onto a New York City building without someone with connections. Bryan has those connections."

Tom looked at me, then at the long road in front of him. He sighed and bent his head forward, eyes closed. "Okay, you win. We go to Bryan's."

"I should probably call him to let him know."

"You should probably not."

"What does it mean to you?" I reached for my percom. In a flash, Tom's left hand tossed it on the back seat.

"Let's break it to him slowly."

"Yeah, right: like he's going to take it any better."

"Ooh! Is that doubt I hear?" Tom laughed.

"Maybe." The word jumped out snappish and harsh.

"See? This is why we shouldn't tell him at all. What makes you think he's going to take it very well?"

"I—"

"The question was rhetorical, Jo. But are you really having second thoughts about whether to see him or not?"

I was. "No." I made it sound as firm as I could, which wasn't at all intimidating.

Resigned, Tom said, "All right then. We're off to see Bryan McQueen."

The car zoomed on.

Bryan's gargantuan apartment complex was lit with the artificial light of the people living inside. The dark blue Charger pulled up into a parking space outlined with strong yellow paint. It looked fresh.

I stepped out of the car and on the curb, waiting for Tom to emerge. He slapped the steering wheel on the top (it was an odd idiosyncrasy), clicked the buckle and opened the door a crack, then shoved it forward, nearly renting it apart from the car.

He joined me on the sidewalk as I strode to the automatic glass doors and walked fast for the elevator. Tom turned toward the staircase.

"Why are you going that way?" I said.

"I want to take the stairs," Tom replied. His voice had false cheeriness to it.

"I'm all for exercise, but we're kind of going to the penthouse—maybe you should reconsider."

Tom rolled his eyes. We stepped into the elevator, and Tom pressed the "P" button.

Ding. The oddly-warped sound filled the small closet of the elevator. The lighting was warm and the whole elevator was spic and span.

Ding. The sound came a second time after a long period of silence. Finally, the door slid open, smooth and perfect-sounding.

The single door sat across the hall from the elevator, which was itself next to the staircase. The penthouse door was clean as anything else in the building.

I expertly knocked on the door in the three specific places, opening it with automatic precision; Tom messed with his dark brown hair and put on a more pleasant yet still serous face than what he had: a rather angry and somewhat pouty emotion.

"Oh gee—BLUE guests!" said Bryan in his husky, New Yorker voice. I stepped forward, the door closing and locking behind Tom, who followed me inside. "I feel unprepared. Would you like me to take you to a pizza joint? I haven't had breakfast, and…"

Bryan's figure emerged into the room. "Oh, it's you! How are you, Agent 12? I heard the news. It must be relieving to be Agent 12 again." He winked.

"Are you kidding?" I said. "Gary's been captured!" My voice almost rose to a yell.

"BLUE will send in someone soon enough, you'll see." Bryan walked over to a couch and sat down.

I took a few steps to face Bryan, who was picking up his keys off of a coffee table beside a couch. "We're already on our way to save him."

"What?" Bryan said. "How can you be going to save Gary Thomson when you don't know where—"

"Where their new base is?" Tom said. He smiled his trademark conspiracy smile. "I know where it is. We both do."

"How? Who authorized...I'm surprised that they would allow you to go this early, with such little evidence. I mean—"

"We're on our way of our own accord," I said. "We got the information and came on our way to get Gary back for the BLUE."

Bryan looked at both of us. "I'm surprised! You two have some excellent nerve to be going to somewhere you don't even know exists."

"Really?" Tom said, also surprised.

"We do know it exists," I said confidently.

"Still I support you fully. I've often been accused of not being...well, serious about the rules of the BLUE. In reality I've been accused of not being legalistic enough, if I could give that board of directors a burning-hot piece of my mind...anyway, what do you two need help with?"

Tom looked at me with a look that said that this would need a lot of explaining. "Maybe we should take you up on that pizza-joint offer."

"Uh...er...all right, then. Do we want to go in my car, or would you prefer your own?"

"I'll go in your car," I said, "and Tom, would you drive yours? I have some things I have to talk to Bryan about one-on-one."

"Um..." Tom was hesitant. I looked at him firmly. "Okay," he said in a rush. He pulled his keys out of his pocket and walked out of the room swiftly and silently. I felt bad for telling him he had to go alone, but there were some things I had to keep between me and Bryan.

Bryan was a rougher driver than Tom. He zoomed through the streets recklessly, and Tom followed behind. Tom drove as if he was very nervous—which he probably was.

"So...I hear you need to talk to me one-on-one?" Bryan said. "What's the dealio?"

"There's something more that's going on here," I said. "We're not just saving Gary."

"I wondered about that. How did you find out where the base was?"

"We received a message via a random CD appearing in Tom's car. We played it—it was a very personalized message. I have no idea how they figured out all the stuff they did. Anyway...it's from a person named JCDO. Deep voice; French. Familiar?"

"Not registering. What else was in the message besides where the base was?"

"It didn't give the location in the message itself. They gave us a website that had the info."

"What was the website?"

"I dunno...I have it on a notepad in Tom's car."

"You should have brought that with you if you were gonna tell me this. Continue."

"They said that they would have a planted representative. I don't know what the heck that means. He said the representative would escort me to discuss some things about our agency."

"It's probably a message from a different corporation than RED or BLUE. Quick question...what did the guy sound like?"

"Already told you...he sounded French."

"That's something, at least. So it might be based in France…but we can't be sure. I'd go with the idea that it's a French independent. So what's the problem in all of this?"

"Well…the thing was, I was notified about this 'discussion' this representative will take us to weeks ago. I was told that I was late for it…he called it 'a negotiation'."

"Wait, wait…stop. Who contacted you about it?"

"A guy named Lewis Trenton. Denise said he was a RED agent, and I gathered that they used to be friends. Do you know anything about him? He's been contacting me for two weeks, but Denise won't say anything about him."

"Ah…Lewis Trenton. That rings a bell. Well, at least, a warning bell. He's one of the slimiest characters at the RED Agency. One of the chief executive's advisors. Really good at foolin' people."

"So maybe this whole thing is a trap?"

"I wouldn't bank on it. It's worth a shot—it doesn't sound like the RED Agency to be able to track conversations in a car and then somehow plant a CD there. It seems to me like there's a third party."

"Any idea who the third party is?"

We were coming up on the pizza place, so I had to get my last question in fast.

"Not one."

"So should we go with the planted representative, see what he says? If Trenton is involved…"

"Don't sweat it. I'm going to have some guys waiting for you outside the RED base. If you have an emergency of any kind, just call me on your percom."

"All right," I said resignedly. The car parallel parked next to the building, Tom pulling up behind us. I wrenched the door open and stepped silently into the restaurant.

"You and Bryan have your little chat?" Tom said. His voice was cold.

"Tom, you don't have to be all bitter about it," I said. Sighing, I sat down in a booth. Tom sat across from me.

"Well, you just make your little secrets with your buddies while I sit over here and watch. Whose idea was this mission?"

"Look…there's more to this than you think, than you know. I had to have someone besides Denise know about it because Denise won't tell me anything."

"So you can talk to Bryan, but not to good ole' Tom?" He got a crooked smile on his face. "Trust me, man. I'm going to find out about whatever this is anyway."

"Yes, you will—once we meet the so-called planted representative. And I think I know who he's representing."

I looked over Tom's shoulder. "Get us a pepperoni, Bryan!"

"Will do."

I scooted over to the edge toward the wall. "No hard feelings, right, Tom?" I tried my best to sound cheery.

"Puh," Tom said, retaining the angry expression on his face.

After a few minutes of awkward silence, Bryan sat down. "It'll only be a couple of minutes—I was just watching them put it in the oven. So, do we want to get down to business?"

Tom looked at me. "Sure," he said. Any trace of the anger from his last conversation was gone, or at least convincingly hidden.

"So this building…how are you going to infiltrate it?"

"That's where you come in," Tom said.

"It'd be best to have a jet," I said. "We need to skydive onto a building here in the city."

A woman with a pizza tray and cutter walked to our table. Setting the tray down, she cut it into eight even slices.

"Thank you!" Bryan said. The waitress walked away in a hurry.

Hungrily I took a large slice of pizza and placed it onto the plate in front of me. It was scalding-hot, as I discovered in a burning bite that scorched the roof of my mouth. Quickly swallowing and grimacing from the burn, I put the slice down.

"So...when do you need this jet?" Bryan had taken his slice and was shaking Parmesan cheese on top.

"Tomorrow night. We need to dive onto a four-foot space at the top of a building. Do you have any guiding technology that we could attach to the top to sort of pull us to the building—guide the armor suits that we brought?"

"I think I have one of those—the LocaFinder. It can guide any object to another object via its two attachable parts that are attracted to each other. And they come with a handy gun that can fire them onto the target precisely. You could launch the guider and then jump. The device would then guide you. Heck, even with a parachute you could work it."

Bryan smiled and folded his slice in half, taking a large mouthful. I accepted this as a signal for me to start eating as well, though my mouth still burned from my first bite.

"Perfect," I said. "So, you can get all this technology in one day?"

"I have connections." Bryan winked. "You can stay in the penthouse. There are plenty of bedrooms to sleep in, so you'll be well accommodated."

"Thanks," Tom said.

I wiped my hand on a napkin, taking time afterward to scratch my arm. "Bryan, should we inform Tom about what we talked about earlier today?"

"I see no reason why not."

Tom looked eager. "So what were you talking about?"

"A couple weeks ago I was contacted by a RED agent—Lewis Trenton. He pretty much predicted that we were going to receive that message, and he said that we would be taken to some sort of delegation or negotiation or whatever," I said.

"That's probably why the CD said that there would be a 'planted representative.' They're going to take you to the delegation, no doubt. And it's a third party." Bryan tore off another bite of pizza and chewed it slowly.

"What do you mean? There's another agency?" Tom said.

"Certainly," said Bryan. "Who else could have contacted you?"

"Do you mind, Bryan? I think I know the name of this agency," I said.

"Do you? Please, do tell."

"Judging by the website, it's called the GREEN Agency."

Bryan suddenly had a stunned look on his face. He quickly swallowed. "The, uh...the GREEN Agency? I don't think you know what you're talking about, Josiah."

"I think I do. On the website, there were three banners—a red, a green, and a blue one. By selecting the red one, we got the RED Agency's profile. I think that if we went to that website again and clicked on the green banner it would take us to this different agency's page."

"Like I said...you don't know what you're talking about. There is a GREEN Agency, I'll admit, but they're not ones to take agents from the BLUE Agency and talk to them in a ne-gotiation format with RED agents."

"Oh really? Where is the GREEN based?"

Bryan was silent for a moment. "Paris."

"What else do you know about the GREEN Agency?"

Tom looked on at us, eyes lost in his own world.

"Nothing. They like to remain a mystery. And perhaps it's a good thing."

Bryan stood up and walked to the counter. I heard him ask for a box, but I didn't care. Who was this agency? What did they stand for? And why were we going to negotiate with them?

"Well, that was rather confusing," Tom said.

"You know," I said, "I think I'm going to drive with you on the way back to the apartment."

"Good idea," Tom said. I took the last bite of my pizza slice and walked out the door, trailing behind Tom.

CHAPTER 6: BREAKING AND ENTERING

The morning came quickly after a deep sleep that night. I woke up, six o'clock exactly. I walked into the kitchen only to find that Bryan had already made chocolate-chip pancakes, exactly the same as the last time I'd visited.

"You must be a fan of pancakes," I said groggily. I picked up a plate and a pair of piping hot cakes.

"So I contacted my pilot last night." Bryan was sitting at the other end of the table eating from a stack of four pancakes on his plate. "He said he'll have it ready in a private airport. If you know what I mean by 'private'."

"Government only."

"Correction: All-Force BLUE only. *That's* something special." Bryan winked, and took another bite of pancake that was slathered with butter, syrup, and whipped cream. I could see an open cabinet that had all of these items stocked in bulk.

"Does he have the other stuff we want?" I said, grin on my face.

"I don't know. He has a lot of stuff, though. I trust Trevor to have a lot. He's one of those technology-obsessed guys. He's on the invention board, you know. Invented the basic idea for the shield!"

"Is he going to be able to fly us there?"

"Let's hope he will!" Bryan laughed. "He's one of the most experienced pilots I've ever met."

Tom walked into the room, his feet clunking on the ground. He wore gym shorts and a white T-shirt.

"About time you came for breakfast."

"Meh, I tried." Tom walked to the table and made a plate of cakes, spreading on maple syrup.

"So…just to fill you in," I said, "Bryan has so graciously booked the flight already. Are we going in a regular jet?"

"Regular jet? Why would a regular jet be All-Force only?" Bryan laughed heartily. "I got you guys a good 'un: Stealth fighter." Bryan swallowed the load of pancake and chocolate in his mouth. "It's a nice-looking plane. I think you're going to like it."

"I hope so. I'd hate to fly in something I didn't like," Tom said. "Would be a shame to jump off of a prop plane."

"That's too dangerous. Besides, you have no stealth with something clunky like that." Bryan wiped his mouth with a white napkin, which now looked like it would never be able to be used again. "This stealth fighter is almost totally silent, no flashy lights—and it's practically invisible."

"What if another plane comes along and runs into it?" I asked.

"You don't think we have radar and notification that

would indicate that long before it happened?" Bryan laughed again.

"Sorry…it's morning. I can't think in the morning."

"So we go tonight, and find out who the heck this Lewis Trenton is," Tom said. "Are you infiltrating with us, Bryan?"

Bryan scratched his chin. "'Fraid not. I'm not the one to ask to do that. But you two can handle it yourselves.

"I…I guess," Tom said. Without another bite, he stood up and walked out. "I'm going to get dressed."

"Strange," I said. *He might have never skydived before. Come to think of it, I've never skydived before. But I think I can handle it…I'm an agent, after all.*

A stealth fighter's wings sliced through the air, quickly, silently. Its black outline was almost completely invisible; no one would ever be able to spot this baby from the ground—even from the top of the RED building.

I sat on a comfortable bench in the belly of the plane, across from Tom and next to Bryan. "Have you ever jumped off one of these, Bryan?"

"Yeah, a couple times. I'm not much into doing the stunts. I like doing the research half of it. I let you guys do the jumping. Of course, I only jumped to make sure you guys were going to be able to land on top of a building."

"What building did you use the technology for?" Tom asked.

"My own apartment complex. No one's going to care that I skydived onto my own building. Besides, there's no way they would be able to know with all the stealth equipment."

"Where do you find the time to do this stuff?" I asked.

"I usually do it at night," Bryan said. "No one notices

when I work in the dark, so that's when you do a lot of practicin' for missions like this one."

Tom looked slightly frightened that we were going to be jumping from such a high altitude. His mouth didn't move, but his eyes, lids and brow told me the whole story.

"Have you ever jumped off a plane, Tom?" I said.

"It's no cakewalk, Josiah."

I hadn't been too jittery before, but now felt a rush of fear flow through me. My spine tingled. "Are you afraid of heights, or something?" My lips quivered.

Tom winced. "That's something that's been around since I was a kid. I didn't like flying on a plane, never mind jumping off of one." Now his voice showed the wavers of fear.

"Come on, Tom," said Bryan. "Take it like a man. You're trying to save Gary here!"

Tom's face didn't change. He alternated between clenching and relaxing his jaw to stop it from shaking.

"So, when should we get there?" Tom asked.

"'Bout five more minutes," Bryan said. He was hunched over, resting his elbow on his knee. "You going to be sick, man?"

"No," Tom said. His lip stopped shaking. Leaning back, he felt at his backpack and parachute as if to make sure they were still there. The reassurance seemed to strengthen him.

"I think I'm ready to jump," Tom said firmly.

"You know, if you really don't want to, I could—" Bryan consoled.

"No. I'm going."

Awkward silence filled the cabin for a few seconds. "Are you two getting a signal from the homing device?" Bryan asked.

"You already checked that ten minutes ago. It's going fine," I said.

All of a sudden, on came the green light. A large hatch opened out of the front and bottom of the plane, slowly revealing the outside world. I put on my sleek black helmet.

I shivered as the blast of air rushed around my body. "Tom, you go first," I said.

Tom nodded, stood up, ran, and leaped from the plane, arms spread. I waited tensely for a few seconds. The green light flashed on once again.

I stood, shaking. Excitement flowed unadulterated through my body. I felt the sheer energy in my muscles, pulsing, beating, and urging them to move.

I ran. The space left on the plane's dark floor was gone too fast. I was on the edge, about to fall. I bounded out, nearly hitting my head on the edge of the doorframe.

The rush of air met me as I descended toward the ground. I felt myself flying, going forward until I was directly above the building. It was a sensation of weightlessness: I was a leaf floating on a pillow of air. My parachute went up. All of it happened so fast—it couldn't have taken more than ten seconds.

I slowly came down, down toward the building. I saw Tom next to me; I could have sworn he was laughing.

The homing device could be seen flashing its small red LED light from the top of the skyscraper. The device guided me downward toward the four-foot space. Tom landed on the top, completely unharmed, not even shaken. The BLUE parachute shot with a slithering slide into his backpack. It was precisely made for a smooth landing.

Gracefully my feet met the three-foot area of glass surrounded by a foot of metal. From there, the top of the building went on at a gentle, then a steep slope, then a sheer drop down to the ground.

Luckily, the area of gentle slope wasn't slippery.

Tom sighed with relief through the grate of the helmet. "Let's get it done."

Water gurgled against the underside of the thick glass on the very top of the building: the central fountain inside and directly below it was tall enough for its water to hit the roof.

"Can you see whether or not Frederick is in there?" I asked.

Tom attempted to survey the small room through the distortion of the water on the glass. "I can't tell. We'll have to take a chance. Guns are in the backpack," he said, patting the black bag. "Just in case, why don't we get them out right now?"

The bag slid off his back and on the narrow area of metal. He zipped it open and removed three black-colored objects. Two stunner pistols (the new model that had recently been released) and a glass cutter now sat on the glass.

"Where'd you get the glass cutter?" I asked.

"I brought one with me. I figured I would need everything possible to break into somewhere, so I've got a lot of stuff. Here." He tossed me one of the pistols.

I holstered the gun, which was cold and light.

"Ehh...you might want to have that out and ready, Jo." Tom dexterously held the cutter in the center of the glass, punched in a few numbers in the keypad and waited.

An arm shot out of the cylindrical black device. Its tip had a laser facing down at the glass, about an inch away from the edge. It rotated around quickly, slicing a perfectly-cut circle and leaving a glowing edge in its path.

The water pushed the cut glass upward slightly. "Here," I

said, pulling the circle off the center and placing it on the edge of the building's top.

"You first," I said.

"No way—I went skydiving first." Tom was putting his backpack on.

I rolled my eyes and placed my gloved hands on the sharp edges of the window, glad that I was wearing thick leather gloves.

Water rushed around me, circling around my suit. It was partially waterproof; only a few drops of water seeped through onto my clothes and ultimately my body. I quickly resisted the flow of water and was deposited onto the floor below me after a quick drop from the fountain.

I slipped, falling on my back. Carefully, slowly I stood. Louder-than-normal sloshing sounds came from the fountain. I moved out of the way as Tom dropped onto the floor gracefully. Water dripped from his skydiving suit to the floor.

"Let's move out," Tom said.

He led the way around the room to a trapdoor. It was unlocked, thank goodness. I dropped to a carpeted hallway floor.

The halls were empty and soundless. No one could have been there. Tom removed his helmet from his backpack and slipped it on; I followed.

The halls were so deathly silent (we made sure not to make a sound as we sneaked through the hallways) that I soon became bored of walking down them.

"So, why are you a conspiracy theorist?" I asked through the helmet percom.

"I'm not usually," Tom said. "I just like to spice things up sometimes."

"From what I hear, this kind of stuff isn't unusual for you."

Tom stopped. "Who told you that?"

"David."

He continued walking and shook his head. "Why would he say that about me?"

"Maybe it's true. Do you really expect me to believe that you've never thought, say, the President was evil or something?"

Tom laughed. "That's now who I am. I like to find back-door ways to think about things. That's what we were trained to do, wasn't it?"

"I guess." Silently we walked. I stared of into space for a while. "What are we looking for now, anyway?"

"Do you remember what floor the detention block was on? It had a map of the building on the website."

"Umm…I think it was the lower basement."

"We need to find an elevator and just hope that there's no one in it."

"Gotcha. It should be on the inner wall, I think."

"That's not good. We don't want to go to the inner part of the building. There could still be RED agents in there."

"Oh, come off it. Here, that's an elevator right there. There won't be any RED agents there at this time of night."

"You can't be sure…"

I pressed "down" on the elevator, and it slid open casually. I half expected it to be full of RED agents, guns drawn, but it was empty.

I hurried in. I might have made a couple of sounds, but no one walked the outside hallway to hear them.

Tom quickly pressed the "B2" button. The doors closed

and the elevator lowered slowly as any elevator down floor after floor. The elevator itself smelled slightly of cigarette smoke.

The door slid open after over a full minute. I stepped into a room that looked like a stairwell, with a circular device on the wall where an exit doorway would be if we were on the ground floor. It looked like an air-conditioning control.

I tried opening the door, which was, of course, locked.

"Here." Tom opened his backpack again and pulled out a blank card. He slid it in the cardkey slot on the door, and it opened silently.

"So that's how we're going to open his cell," I said to myself. Tom laughed until I gave him a look, at which he immediately subsided.

Tom was first to walk into the long hall with cells on either side. The cells themselves had walls of translucent material. I could see everyone inside. They were all asleep—not one noticed us entering.

"Shields up," Tom said.

Both our shields flickered into existence, casting the faintest blue light on the otherwise dim corridor.

My pistol was drawn, safety off, my trigger finger shaking. The detention block was grimly silent. I felt darkness seeping over my body—a dark hostility covered the room.

There was no Gary in sight yet…he had to be in one of these small and uncomfortable-looking cells. I hurried faster and faster, looking on both sides of me for Gary. Tom was doing the same—he wasn't in any we had seen yet. We were nearing the end of the hallway; I feared we had come here for nothing—we were sure to get caught anyway.

Then I saw it…he was here. The person whom I had thought was dead was now sleeping twenty feet away from me, cell 7336. Carelessly, I ran toward the cell with the key in my hand. I pounded on the surface of the cell. It was hard and cold—it made resonating, deep sounds each time I hit it with my hand.

Gary jolted awake. He rubbed his eyes, looked at me, my BLUE uniform...he looked utterly joyful. At least, for a moment.

I reached to slide the keycard into the slot when I felt something cause my shield to ripple. I looked over my shoulder and saw a RED agent with his hand on my shoulder. No big surprise.

I smacked him in his unshielded face, giving him a nice shock of energy from my shield's electrical field. I watched Tom brandish his gun as seven more RED agents came from somewhere above us.

"Josiah! Don't hesitate! Fire!"

The RED agents leapt toward us and sent a flurry of bolts our way, which I blocked with my shield. I returned the shots with my gun.

I found myself face-to-face with another RED agent, who quickly fell, unconscious, to the ground, only to be replaced by another. They seemed to be multiplying—we were outnumbered at least five-to-one now. This RED agent flicked his carbine around and pounded my shield repeatedly. The first few times it merely bounced off, but soon my shield was weakening, and I was having a harder time shooting back. He was stealing its power.

I saw the same thing happening to Tom. I tried to fire, but I was rejected. My shield was down. I saw the barrel of the gun....

I felt myself go into shock, then float into a sequence of

strange dreams....

I felt myself slip off to sleep. I was unconscious. We had failed.

CHAPTER 7: PRISON BREAK

When I woke up, I was lying on a small cot, my feet hanging off the edge. I looked over and saw Tom talking quietly yet adamantly to someone...he was lying on his own cot....

I sat up and remembered where we were. Gary sat on the cot furthest from me, having a conversation with Tom. He stood gave a strong hug, letting go quickly.

"Gary! We thought you were dead!" I said.

"I live on," Gary said with a smile.

"Have you cracked? Leaked? Told anything?" Tom asked.

"Of course not," Gary said. "You question my loyalty?"

"Not necessarily," Tom said, sitting up from his cot, then standing up completely.

"Then why did you ask?" Gary asked him, confused.

"It was just for security," Tom said, mumbling.

"Let's move on, shall we?" I said. "How do we plan on

getting out of here? We don't really have a plan, and I don't see any immediate flaws in the design of the building. I think we're going to be stuck here for a while."

"We told Bryan to be waiting outside with some other agents, didn't we?" Tom said.

"Yeah, we did, but I don't see how that's going to help. We've had a heck of a time getting in here, and they're going to have the same luck, I'm guessing." I shifted in my cot. "Besides, how are we going to contact him without our stuff?"

"Don't worry. It isn't going to be a life and death thing if we stay here for a little while," Gary said.

"How is it not going to be a life and death thing?" Tom said. "We need to get out of here. They'll probably have no reason to keep us once they've picked our brains for information. Easiest way to dispose of us is to kill us."

"Don't be irrational," Gary said.

"I'm being perfectly rational!"

"Who said that they were going to get any information from us?"

"Even if they don't," Tom said darkly, "they'll still have no use for us when they're done interrogating."

"We can get out of here soon then," Gary said lightly and with finality. "And if we die, then we will know that we have died fighting for America and the BLUE Agency."

Tom sighed. "Whatever happened to the GREEN's planted representative? Anyway, let's talk about something else," he said quietly.

"Yes, I was wondering something…did you ever finish your biography of your sister?" I asked.

"As a matter of fact…" Gary bent down and reached under his cot for a stack of neat-looking papers and handed them to me. "This is the last part of the book. I finished it here when I was bored, which happens all the time."

"Can you talk to the other prisoners?" I asked.

"No. We're only allowed to see them," Gary said. "This place is terrible."

"Did you try to escape?" I hoped that he hadn't.

"No, that would have been a foolish idea. How would I have done it anyway? There's nothing we could have done to this material." He pointed to the transparent glassy wall.

I thought for a second. "How did you write the book?" I asked. "Where did you get..." I pointed to the paper.

"They loaned me a pen and paper," he said. "A couple of them aren't that cruel."

"Wouldn't they worry about you killing yourself with the pen?" I joked, puzzling over his last statement.

Gary smiled for a second. "That stuff only happens in movies. They'd find a way to keep me from dying."

"I'm glad you were able to write in your sister's memory," Tom said. It sounded like a slick subject change.

"Well," Gary said, "I'd better get to sleep. Got to catch some Z's before tomorrow's interrogation."

"Interrogation?" I said.

"Yeah, we have an interrogation tomorrow," Gary said. "Scheduled it last-minute after you guys arrived."

Without another word, he slipped under his thin cot blanket and fell asleep quickly. I found the room chilly and shivered slightly under my blanket. *My first interrogation tomorrow...and probably not the last.*

I was jolted awake.

Looking around and sitting up, I felt dreary and drowsy.

I rubbed my eyes. Had I heard a sound? If not, I was very un-happy to have woken myself up so early. It couldn't have been more than two hours after I had fallen asleep.

I looked through the glass wall of the cell. Nothing could be seen. Perhaps I had been imagining, a dream, maybe....

But then I heard a loud sound as if someone was being hit. I saw a fist jutting out on the right edge of the wall and a RED guard falling to the ground, out cold.

A stranger to whom the fist belonged stepped in front of the glass. I could barely see him through the dim lighting. He bent down and pilfered a card from the pocket of the RED guard he had taken out. He slid the card into the slot for our cell, and suddenly the whole glass wall slid into the ceiling.

Finally I stood up, looked around: Gary and Tom were just waking up from the sound of the glass wall going up. The stranger stood no more than five-foot-six. His gaze darted from one person to the other.

"Up! We have no time for dawdling..." The stranger's voice was sharp and quiet.

Tom and Gary were fully awake now and standing up. "Who sent you?"

The stranger beckoned and began to walk down the hall. I hurried after him, Tom and Gary beside me. Since the hall-way was almost at an end at this side of the detention area, I wondered where he was going. There was one small door at the end, also with a keycard lock. The stranger effortlessly opened the door with the keycard.

I followed him in, keeping the door open to make sure none of the others were left outside. The stranger looked like he was a BLUE prisoner as well, but certainly didn't operate like a BLUE agent. He used the keycard once again to open a several large lockers against the wall in this small, dim room just like the others.

I looked behind me. Tom looked calm and ready for anything, whereas Gary, clutching his stack of pages, looked like he had just seen a ghost, perhaps one of a duck the size of a school bus.

"You'll need these," said the stranger, tossing Tom and I our backpacks. "And put your regular clothes on."

For the first time, I realized I was adorned with a dirty white shirt and mud-brown shorts. I opened my backpack and donned a clean pair of jeans, a BLUE code shirt (one that didn't say BLUE, but bore the logo on it) and my black jacket.

"Gary, you'll need your weapons." The stranger handed Gary his shield, belt, and carbine. "They're all outdated, but please bear with me. And you can borrow some of my clothes; I think they'd fit you."

He reached into the third locker and tossed a pair of plain-looking blue jeans and a lime-green polo with a symbol I had never seen embroidered to the front. He then took out his own suitcase.

By this time, everyone was wearing normal clothes and our prison attire was thrown into a sad-looking pile on the ground. I zipped up my backpack and slung it over my back. The rest of my stuff was still with Bryan…we needed to contact him.

"Off to Paris, then," said the stranger casually.

"Wait," I said.

The stranger did not wait—he walked out the door and down the hallway, bag hanging over his back. *This must be the representative, I know it!*

"Paris?" Tom asked, incredulous.

"All in good time, Tom. We've got to get to JFK first. I have four tickets beside my own. I thought Bryan might want to come with us." The stranger's voice remained extremely casual as he walked past a RED agent who looked like he was regaining consciousness, and then swerved around a cluster of other REDs who were still unconscious, one with a bleeding nose, another with a broken lip.

"How did you get…how did you defeat all these guys?" My mind was still in the RED base.

"With great precision. And lots of practice."

I don't want to know who he practiced on.

At the end of the hall, he opened the stairwell door, this time without even sliding the keycard in. Instead of going into the elevator or up the steps, he walked to the circular device on the opposite wall that looked like the air conditioning control.

He twirled it swiftly with his right hand, and suddenly it opened like a door to a tunnel. He stepped in without a word.

As I walked in looking around, I realized that this tunnel was made entirely of marble. The floor was a beautiful green-colored marble with swirls of bright yellow; the walls and ceiling were of pearl-colored marble with swirls of green.

The passage ended in a light, making the stranger fully visible for the first time. He stepped into the light, which happened to be an open doorway to the parking lot outside. I stepped onto the blacktop and looked behind me. We walked out of a storage shed with a crude door that had an old Masterkey padlock on it.

A lone car set in a parking space. It was green, had no car brand on it, and had hubcaps with the same strange design as on Gary's polo engraved in the center.

"Well," said the stranger as we all stood at the car, "I am Broc James, and I have been sent to be your escort. Josiah, you have shotgun. Gary, you get com seat. Tom, you sit behind Josiah."

Him calling us by first names made me uneasy.

I stepped around the back of the car, hurled the door open, and sat with a soft *thud* that was lost in the cushion. It was comfortable and there was plenty of legroom, but this did not ease my confusion. I shut the door and clicked the seat belt buckle.

I looked over at Broc. He appeared taller in the car than he had in the RED base. The driver's seat seemed suited to his stature—a smaller steering wheel, pedals closer to his feet, and the headrest lowered to accommodate for his height.

He leaned forward. His nose, now nearly touching the steering wheel, was as sharply pointed as his speech, and his strawberry-blond hair hung just over his eyebrows. Stretching a short arm, he turned the key. The car started up immediately, but you almost couldn't tell because it was so quiet.

As the car began to pull out of the parking lot, Tom said, "So who are you anyway?"

I saw a wry smile form on Broc's face. "Broc James."

"Who are you working for, I mean. Are you JCDO?" Tom replied snappily. Although he seemed awake, he was clearly not happy he was awoken so early. *He could be a bit more grateful...after all; Broc did save us from the RED.*

"I work for...well, I guess you could call them the GREEN Agency." The car drove down the street and toward the airport. "I only have a short time to explain, so please give me all your questions now." He now sounded hurried.

"And who is the GREEN Agency?" I asked. *I knew it.*

"You'll find that out in Paris. It's not my job to tell you," Broc said in a rush. He pushed the pedal down harder.

"Then whose job is it?" Tom said. "JCDO's? And who is JCDO, anyway?"

"He's our military general."

"And what does JCDO stand for?" I asked.

"You can find out when you meet him. You'll be seeing quite a lot of him, since he's going to be negotiating with you. Is that all your questions?"

"Yes," Tom said.

"No," Gary retorted. "I still have no idea what we're talking about."

"Remember what I told you about the car ride here?" Tom said. "Well, they told us there would be the planted representative and I think this is him."

"Ah," Gary said.

"Yes, I am the planted representative the message referred to. In fact, I planted that message."

"How did you—" I was interrupted.

"We have no time for trivial questions like this. We need to get a move on. Tom, you have com seat. Call Bryan, tell him that Gary is all right, and tell him that he needs to meet us at JFK." Broc swerved around a turn, pushing down the pedal even faster as we whizzed past yellow taxis and large white buses.

Tom picked up his percom and I heard him say both to Bryan. I also heard sounds of happiness from the other line as Tom relayed how they had gotten Gary out alive and safe, then a quieter mumble as he was told to come to JFK.

I looked out the window at the tall buildings and crowded sidewalks of New York City. *How did this GREEN Agency know all this? And how did he plant that message? I guess we'll have to find out once we reach our destination.*

CHAPTER 8: PARIS

The car didn't lurch as it pulled into a parking space at JFK. The instant it went into park I was out the door, ready for whatever Broc wanted us to do.

Broc didn't give any instructions or even say anything, just began walking through the parking garage. The three of us trailed behind so we could discuss the current turn of events.

"Did you expect anything like this, Tom?" I asked.

"Not at all." Tom was walking fast for him—his gait was usually a slow one.

"I'm just along for the ride, I guess," Gary said.

"No…you're apparently an important piece in this new game," I said. "The RED wanted you and they're not going to be happy that we stole you back."

"How does this tie in with that Trenton guy?" Tom looked at me.

I had been so focused on the situation at hand that I had

totally forgotten about Lewis Trenton. "I don't know…" My voice trailed off. "Both he and Broc said something about a negotiation, so maybe…"

No time remained to finish our conversation—we were at the glass doors, and Broc was waiting emotionlessly. He pulled the entrance open and we followed close behind him this time.

The weight of my backpack was beginning to set in, the straps digging into my shoulders. I swung it off and carried it with one arm. Just as well, because we were coming up to the metal detectors.

Broc stopped us with his hand before we could go through the detectors. Broc pulled his wallet out of his back pocket and took out a round card. Placing his wallet back, he stepped over to the security guard and showed him the card. He nodded and let us through, ignoring the fact that the sensors went off like crazy.

"You'll need to put those in the cargo bay, though," said the security guard as we walked past.

"I was planning on it." Broc said without turning.

I stared at Broc. "What was that all about?"

"I merely certified that we were on…official business and that we needed to take our weapons over the border on a commercial flight." Broc quickened his step, and I could se why. Bryan was standing near the first terminal, holding in his left arm Tom's bag that also carried my luggage.

"About time you kids got here," said Bryan, ignoring the fact that he was only fifteen. "I've gotten a bit sick of standin' around."

"You couldn't have been here that long," Tom said. "I called you just a few minutes ago."

"I have my ways." Bryan chucked Tom's bag in his direction; Tom caught it despite the throw's bad aim.

"So, you coming with?" Gary said.

"Certainly. Who's your little buddy here?" Bryan smiled and patted Broc on the shoulder with a heavy hand. Broc seemed unfazed by being called "little".

"Broc James." Broc had to tilt his head up to look Bryan in the eye. "I'm with Grandpa—he'll be waiting for us when we get there."

"Ah," said Bryan, long and slow. "Well, that's good. So you're not Trenton?"

"I retrieved Trenton quite a while ago," Broc said. "But we needn't talk business when our flight starts so soon."

The conversation left me uninformed, but I got as much to know that Grandpa meant the GREEN Agency.

Broc led us to our terminal and we just walked on the plane after briefly showing the card to the ticket collector outside.

We were definitely flying in style.

Five seats were in the center row, three on either side. It was an airbus, and we had first-class seats in a center row. I was a bit disappointed that I couldn't sit by the window and watch the plane take off, but all the same it would be a bit unnerving to look out on the depths of the ocean and imagine plunging into the water as the plane exploded or something.

I took my seat next to the end of the row. An aisle seat. Tom stood on my right. "Do you mind if I sit here?" he asked.

"Not at all."

Tom sat down and leaned the chair back.

"They're going to ask you to have your seat in the upright

position in twenty minutes anyway."

Tom said nothing and kept his seat back. I looked in front of me once again. The flight attendant had taken her position in welcoming everyone who entered the airbus.

Broc sat down next to me at the end of the row once he had made sure everyone else was sitting down. I felt uncomfortable—he wasn't my buddy or Tom's anything. The uneasiness increased when he turned his head looked at me expressionlessly, and looked forward again.

Attempting to ignore this, I watched as the plane filled row by row with talkative passengers.

I felt the plane lurch. For the first time in my life I was leaving the country. I had just realized that I had always been in the United States...now I was going somewhere different. I remembered that I had always wanted to leave America, to go somewhere in Europe. Somewhere like Paris.

"Josiah."

A cold, bony hand lifted me from my seat in the plane. I was instantly awake and aware that Broc had his hand on my shoulder and that everyone else in our row was exiting the plane. I shook my head, hair flying, and followed Broc, who was not letting go of my shoulder. He had to stretch his arm to reach it, and it looked rather ridiculous from the outside (or so Gary says).

After that I zoned out—I'm pretty sure Broc had let go of me, but I didn't notice when he did. I mindlessly followed him, not paying attention to the hushed conversation Tom and Gary were having with Bryan. The airport whizzed by me like I was a ghost.

Once we exited, I became aware that we were somewhere

totally unfamiliar, judging by the Eiffel Tower jutting out of the skyline.

"Where do we go now?" I asked.

"To eat." Broc walked silently along the sidewalk. He jumped into the same sort of car we had driven to JFK in.

Once I sat shotgun, I realized it was the same car.

"Some kind of café or something?" Bryan asked. "We have some of those in New York. In fact, I know a great one called—"

"We don't have time, this is it," said Broc. He pulled up at a small, clean, stone building that had a sign that said "Écouter." I had taken a French class earlier in life, but I didn't know what this meant.

"What does Écouter mean?" I asked in a whisper to Tom after exiting the car.

"To listen to, perhaps an espionage reference." He looked confused at why there would be a café called To Listen To.

"Hm..." I said. "Do you think it could be a GREEN-owned café?"

"Probably," Tom said.

The door swiveled open though no one touched it, and Broc led us into a cozy one-room operation with several tables and chairs set against a wall and one round table in a small cove surrounded by green, puffy armchairs. There was a small counter behind which was a swinging metal door.

"What do we want? Any sandwich combination you can think of, they'll have it here." Broc stood in front of the counter.

"Ham, Swiss, and lettuce," I said.

Broc relayed it to the waiter behind the counter (who had a peculiar mustache) in perfectly fluent French—he almost sounded like he was a local. Broc then returned to an American accent to talk to Tom about his order.

I sat in one of the green armchairs. Soon the others hustled themselves over to our table, food in hand. Gary slid me my sandwich—the artisan bread was warm and the cheese was melting when I bit in.

"So," Broc said, chewing a mouthful of sandwich, "we wait for our message here. They'll slide it to us via our receipt. It'll have all our information we need."

The mustached waiter stepped out from behind the counter and set a steaming cup of coffee in front of each person.

"What kind of information is in the receipt?" Bryan asked, sipping his coffee. He looked surprised that it was any good.

"The GREEN Agency has ways of getting into the base that are…complicated," Broc said.

Bryan almost spewed his coffee all over the place, but instead swallowed hard. "Sh! Don't talk about that here! There could be—"

"It doesn't matter. The GREEN own this restaurant," Broc said. "Often we have to get in through unsuspecting places. I once had to put my hand into a mailbox and grab what looked like a spider and her egg sac. And they actually moved too…but it was just a key."

I shuddered at this statement and finished eating my sandwich, which I now felt like vomiting all over the table. I soon forgot about the spider key, however, because the waiter, who seemed to be in quite a rush, handed Broc the receipt and rushed out into the kitchen.

"Hmm…" said Broc.

"What does it say?"

"*JAMES:*

"Go to the Eiffel Tower. Be no later than 12:17 by Josiah Jones's watch, 6:17 Paris time. Your runner will be there. He'll wait under the tower at the southern leg. He will be looking at you, facing north, carrying a brown paper shopping bag.

"Stare right at him and use the signal to tell him that you are the one he's looking for. He will drop his shopping bag and leave the tower. You are to run as quickly as you can to the shopping bag. Inside you will find a box, which you should open with a penknife. Inside you will find a metal container sealed with clay. Break the seal and look at the key. The number on the key will tell you what entrance to go to, and you will use the key to open the entrance.

"I wish you luck, ambassador.

"JCDO."

The entire letter totally blew over my head by the time he had finished, but Broc immediately took a cigarette lighter out of his pocket and burned the receipt. "Let's go."

"Don't you need to memorize that?" Gary stood up.

"Already did." Broc hurried out of the restaurant and everyone else tried to keep up, me hobbling along in the back with my backpack still over my back.

CHAPTER 9: GREEN

In only a few minutes, we were at the Eiffel Tower. As promised, a tall, gangling man in a business suit and green tie stood at the southern leg, holding a brown bag. Broc stared at the man directly across and gave a quick hand signal. As promised, the man threw the bag to the ground and bolted away from the tower.

Broc ran faster than I had seen anyone run to the shopping bag. He cut open the box, broke the seal, and was heading toward the entrance before I reached the southern leg.

I soon caught up to Broc now that he was just walking. "Can we just get a quick lowdown on who the GREEN Agency is?"

"No," Broc said flatly. "You'll get your explanation at the base."

I shook my head. The walk was long to the GREEN entrance, but when we made it, I was sorely disappointed.

The entrance was a shoddy house with the siding coming off and the roof almost devoid of shingles. The door was peeling and said "NOT FOR SALE" in spray-painted letters across it. In smaller letters it said "Le Écouter: Number E4".

Broc just stood there, hands on his hips.

"You led us to an abandoned house?" Tom said.

Wordlessly Broc jumped the crumbling cement stairs and gently pressed the key into the lock and turned it quickly. The door swung open.

I jumped the stairs and followed Broc inside, Tom, Gary and Bryan following me. I walked up the stairs after Broc to see that at the top, there was a large wall and nothing else but another air conditioning control wheel.

Broc spun it and the whole wall slid open to reveal a large, sparkling white elevator with buttons lining the whole back wall of it. It was out of place in the dank, creaky house.

Broc stepped in, and the rest of us clambered inside. I raised my eyebrows at how many people could fit in without it being crowded—I had several feet of room to myself.

Broc pressed the bottom-left corner button on the back wall, and without warning, the elevator shot down with such speed that I almost hit my head on the ceiling. Luckily, the ceiling was padded so if that happened you wouldn't break anything vital such as the spine or cranium.

The elevator then shot forward with the speed of a bullet. Instantly it stopped, and I realized that the ride had only taken seconds. I had an intense shaking feeling about me, but this soon dissipated, because when I stepped out of the elevator, I was in the largest and most beautiful room I had ever seen.

Green lights lined the walls and pointed downward, lighting sleek metal benches in with a weird neon feeling. The roof was paneled with huge panes of glass. This was the only part of the building that was out of the ground. Light bathed the entire place from the sun. I could see lights on the metal rafters that held the glass together.

I looked around in amazement. People rushed about, many in black business suits with green ties like the man at the Tower, and others with military uniforms. In the center of the room was the Agent Receiving Desk, or so said the sign hanging above it from no visible place—it simply floated in midair. Several people stood behind the desk, talking to people who needed to be helped and paging the people they needed with their own sleeker version of a personal communicator.

I felt awkward rolling my white luggage bag around and carrying a large black backpack over my shoulders. My casual clothes felt like they stood out now. The people who were in the GREEN Agency were dressed sleekly and talked in quick, professional, no-nonsense tones like Broc. At the BLUE, we would meander around and joke with each other. This was like the total opposite.

Broc stepped in front of the Agent Receiving Desk, where a receptionist with a pale face and heavy makeup stood waiting for him. "What do you need, James?"

"We need to see Jean Claude de Oulaire," he said quickly. "We have the BLUE delegates."

"All right then, I'll call him up." The woman hurriedly clicked on her percom several times. "We have the BLUE delegates, Oulaire. Great. I'm sending them up." She clicked off the personal communicator. "Up to floor 2. Room 299. You know the way, James."

"Right." Broc nodded and gestured with his small hand for us to follow him toward another elevator that was at the very end of the long room. It took us a half a minute to get to the green-lit elevator.

Another less frightening elevator ride later, we arrived right in the office of Jean Claude de Oulaire.

The door opened. I looked around—not very interesting. A desk was in one corner, with multiple papers strewn in disorganized piles, and a state of the art wall monitor (larger than a TV) that the desk was facing. No one sat at the computer's keyboard, though.

Instead, in the center of the room sat a man who looked very tense in one of the same kind of armchairs that we had seen at Le Écouter. We were looking at the back of his head; a buzz cut barely tinting the top of head with a slight amount of light blond hair. His head came far above the back of the armchair.

"Who is it? Is this the delegates from the BLUE Agency? I certainly hope so." The man, whose voice I recognized as JCDO (which must have stood for Jean Claude de Oulaire) held a thick French accent and a strong, overbearing tone, the other extreme to the short and professional speech of the other GREEN agents we had passed by in the gargantuan lobby.

Oulaire stood and turned around. He was a man who was taller than any I had ever seen. He had to be at least six-foot-seven or eight. He only looked about twenty-five years old—perhaps it was the haircut.

"It is," Broc said, who looked microscopic in comparison to the giant figure of Oulaire.

"Good, then. We shall speak right away." Oulaire smiled.

"Bryan, Gary, Tom, Josiah, this is Jean Claude de Oulaire. He is our military general here at the GREEN Agency." Broc gave out his hand to shake Oulaire's.

Oulaire nodded his head and strode toward us. He stretched out his hand to meet mine. His grip was harsh, firm, cold.

He went on to shake hands with the other three, and took a long step back. "Broc, if you will," Oulaire said.

Broc nodded slowly, then walked back in the elevator.

Oulaire walked into a small lounge-like area that I hadn't noticed before in the corner opposite his desk and seated himself in the largest chair. "Come. Sit."

Bryan, Gary, and Tom rested on the couch across from Jean. I sat in another green armchair beside the couch.

Oulaire twiddled his thumbs, going over what he was to say in his mind. "It has come to my attention," he said slowly, "that you are at war with the RED Agency."

"Haven't we always?" I said.

Oulaire looked at me as if I had said something very intelligent. "Yes, you have. Do you know how the GREEN Agency was started?"

"Yes," Bryan said. "The War of 1812. You were trying to keep peace between the British and the French."

How does he know that? I looked at Bryan with surprise.

"Exactly. That's what we've always been about." He leaned back. "Peacemaking between warring sides. The recent actions between you and the RED Agency have been rather—rash."

"Rash, you say?" Gary asked. "And all about peace from the chief executive of the GREEN military?"

Oulaire was silent on the second comment. "Your demolishing of their base, for example," he said. "Completely unnecessary. And then they rebelled not once, but twice, and on the second time they captured a BLUE agent. It was this that we, the members of the Council at the GREEN Agency, knew that we had to act before more drastic things happened on either side."

"And? What did they rule?" Tom asked.

"They ruled that we must send delegates from both sides to our headquarters right here in Paris. We need to resolve the issues you two are having as soon as possible to stop the fighting between both sides."

My mind revolted. *Who do they think they are to stop the RED and BLUE from fighting? The only way to do that is to disable one of the groups, which we have tried to do unsuccessfully to do with the RED. We simply have to get rid of them and the problem will end.* "It isn't that simple. This is not a squabble over any land or anything like that. It's a major international crime syndicate that needs to be stopped. There are ties of these people with the Mafia, MS-13, almost every large organized crime group in the world. You can't solve this problem through *negotiations*," I said.

"This may be an exception to the rules, Josiah Jones," Oulaire said, teeth clenched.

"Do you have the RED delegate here?" Tom asked.

"Yes, but you are not to meet with Trenton until I…we… finish talking here. We need to resolve some important issues this very day."

"How are we supposed to conduct negotiation without both—or in this case all three—sides present?" Bryan said. "We need to have an open discussion between all of us if we're gonna have a fair outcome."

I sighed. *It's more complicated now. There's another agency involved. And I'm not taking this crap that they're not going to take sides.*

"I can concede to have a meeting tonight. But right now

I need you to contact your agency and tell them what's been going on so far in our meeting. I'll call Josiah's percom when it's time for dinner," Oulaire said. He paused for a long time. "Dinner is the first negotiation. Good day."

"So we can't leave?" I said, standing.

"I would ask you to not leave the GREEN headquarters without prior permission," Oulaire said. "You will be taken to your rooms immediately."

"But Mr. Oulaire—"

"Good day."

CHAPTER 10: DINNER

We were escorted to a hotel-like room—two of them, actually. Nicer than the RED facility, still felt like prison.

I was in a room with Tom. He was just lying on the bed, looking up at the green-tinted ceiling, and wondering why we had jumped into this mess. "Are you going to contact D?"

"Yeah...though I don't see much point in it." I picked up my personal communicator, which had been sitting on my pillow since we entered and dialed DTOP, Agent D's percom code.

Agent D picked up. I left the percom on speaker and again laid it to rest on my pillow.

She didn't even bother to say hello.

"Josiah Jones," she said and sighed. "You are one heck of a kid. What do you think you and Tom were doing, going out to rescue Gary?"

"It was Tom's idea."

"I regret it!" Tom said. He was lying on his bed, hands behind his head.

"Anyway…it's a long story. I don't have time to tell you the whole thing right now, but we're in an important situation here." I sat down on the bed, jostling the percom from its spot on the pillow. It fell face forward onto the mattress. I turned it back over quickly.

"What is it?" Denise sounded excited and less condemning now. "Please say something interesting—I'm bored to tears here."

"There's more than just BLUE and RED involved in this battle now," I said.

"Who else is in on it? Do you still think the CIA is a separate entity from the BLUE?" I could almost see her rolling her eyes at me.

"No," I said. I wanted to stay businesslike. This wasn't a time for friendship. "Denise, there's another agency."

"What?" she said. She was rather caught of guard, which in turn surprised me. I thought she would have already known by now.

"The GREEN Agency, they call themselves. You didn't know about this? It would seem that someone would have picked up on them by now."

"I can search the records. Hold up."

I heard her put her end of the percom down, then the clicking of keys while she searched for any BLUE records of the GREEN Agency.

"She's not going to find anything," Tom said.

"She might."

Denise picked up her percom again. "Nope. No record of the GREEN Agency. Anything else you need on the database while I have it open."

"No," Tom said.

I looked at him, surprised at his answer. "Uh, ignore Tom. Yes, we do. I need Jean Claude de Oulaire."

"What? Who's that?"

"He works for the GREEN Agency. Military general. He spoke with us today—and for some reason called us the 'delegates' of the BLUE. Just look him up."

"How do you spell that name?" she asked.

"No idea. Did you see anything suggesting the spelling, Tom?"

"Nameplate on the desk read J-e-a-n C-l-a-u-d-e d-e-O-u-l-a-i-r-e."

I already heard Denise typing into the database. "We've got something on him," she said.

"Really?" I asked. I stood. "What have we got?"

"Jean Claude de Oulaire. Born and resides in France, knows much information about both RED and BLUE Agencies—former employee of the BLUE; worked as a low-ranking general," Denise said. "No wonder we haven't heard of him. He was a nominal member of the BLUE."

"We've got another one. Bookmark Oulaire's page."

"Who else does she need to find?" Tom asked.

"All right, what's next?" she said.

"Broc James." I paced back and forth across the room at the feet of the two beds, anxious, excited.

"Hmm…used to work as a Secret Service member under the alias of Eli Cope. He was found to have faked his name and was fired from the position."

"Interesting," I said. "Maybe he was out for information and let something slip about who he was."

"Later he was shot in the chest and presumed to be dead," Denise continued.

"Whoa…he's certainly not dead. And that's probably the same Broc James that we're thinking about, because—"

"Be quiet, why don't you? He is known by the BLUE to be alive and well, making a quiet residence in Paris, France."

"Definitely the one we're looking for," Tom said. "So he posed as a secret service officer—what president?"

"Clinton. He's 21 years old. Faked his age in 1998 and must have been getting some info. That was part of the reason why he was fired," Denise said.

"Bookmark that page, too," I said.

"Yes." More typing. "Now, I understand that you have some information to give me—it sounds like a lot happened in the past couple of days. What about this GREEN Agency is important and what did they tell you?"

"They led us to the new RED base in New York. We infiltrated and ended up getting locked up in there. Once inside, however, Broc, posing as a BLUE prisoner, busted us out with Gary."

"He was just a prisoner, then?" Denise said.

"So it would seem. He then took us along with Bryan McQueen to Paris and to talk with Jean Claude, a meeting that we just got back from. That's where we are now."

"What did they want to talk with you about?" Denise's voice was wary and suspicious.

"We're supposed to be negotiating peace between us and the RED Agency. They have a delegate here too," I said. Sitting back down, I kicked off my shoes, looking at the clock on the nightstand. *Hurry it up….*

"Pfft. Like they're going to give up that easy. I hate negotiations."

"I know. That's what I thought, too. We're going to have to win this by persuading the GREEN to join the BLUE side. We're supposed to have a dinner with all of us tonight."

"Who's all of us?" Denise asked.

"Me, Jo, Bryan, Gary, Oulaire , and the RED delegate," Tom listed.

"How did Bryan get there? Anyway, I need one of you to come back to the BLUE HQ to help me resolve all this. We were going to call a meeting about all this the day after your little midnight escape, but our primary attendees were missing. This will complicate things a little bit, as will the fact that Gary is now proven to be alive and has been taken back. Send me Bryan and I'll send you another agent as a replacement. Okay?"

"Got it. I'll have Oulaire or Broc contact you about getting the new agent in. Trust me, it's gonna be a long process."

"I'll take your word for it. Contact me with any information you might have, and on the next communication I should have the agent selected and prepared for the mission at a moment's notice."

"Gotcha. Over and out."

"Goodbye, Jones."

The percom beeped, signaling the end of the message. *Now I just have more questions than ever.*

The four of us walked into the private dining room, eight o'clock. The doors closed behind us without a sound. At the end of the table sat Jean Claude de Oulaire. He stood and nodded his head to greet us. He even had a small smile on his face. It looked genuine, but who knew whether it was or not.

"Good day to you, BLUE agents," said Oulaire. He sat, signaling for where we were to sit. The RED delegate sat on the other end of the table, eyebrows raised slightly, next to the end. He looked exactly as I had envisioned him—sharp and biting, with large eyes and small pupils and a small, pointed nose.

I sat down beside Oulaire, greeting him with a friendly handshake. A waiter, finely dressed, walked in through a sliding door I hadn't seen that was on the wall behind Oulaire. The man had a mustache that looked exactly like the one we had seen at the café. In fact, I could have sworn he was the same person. He dropped a menu in front of me.

"I will be right back with drinks—what do we want this evening?" said the waiter, who was obviously French by the sound of his voice. He looked at Oulaire expectantly.

"I'll have the house lemon," he said. "Fresh and cold, no pulp, bottled."

"And you?" He looked at Trenton

"Same as him," Trenton said in his short, clipping tone.

The waiter looked to me.

"What should I get?" I asked Oulaire.

"I recommend the house sodas—there's lemon, lime, strawberry, tangerine, and blue."

"What's blue? What flavor is it?"

"Blue," he said calmly and quite lucidly.

"All right, I'll try blue, then," I said.

"We'll have the same as he is," said Bryan, who was sitting next to me.

"So, two lemons and four blues? All ice-cold bottled, correct?"

I nodded yes.

"All right, then—those will be out in a couple of minutes." The waiter smiled and walked into the door with the same rush he had had at the café.

Where does the GREEN get money for extraneous things like a fancy private kitchen? Well, Denise has the Seclab at the BLUE, but that was from her own pocket....

"Now, on to business. We have a delegate from the RED Agency and four delegates from the BLUE Agency." Oulaire was revealing the smile as a façade.

"How were the BLUE allowed four delegates?" asked Trenton. He was looking at me, eyes blank.

"The only true delegate here is Josiah Jones, but the others wished to come here as well."

"Actually," I said, "Bryan is needed back at the BLUE Agency, and we'll be sending a replacement delegate to take his position here."

"Why do you need a replacement?" Oulaire asked.

"It's not in my hands—it was by order of Agent D," I said.

Oulaire paused and folded his hands. "Well, then, let's continue, shall we?"

The waiter stepped to the table once again and distributed cold glass bottles of soda, dripping with condensation. Two were cloudy yellow and the other four were a translucent blue. I twisted open the bottle and took a swig.

It did taste like blue, but I couldn't put a finger on how.

"As I have already stated, the outbreak of skirmishes has gone on for too long. The GREEN Agency has seen both sides, and many of our cameras were destroyed in the battles, which are not cheap."

Why is he talking like they're poor?

"And then we had to do another rigging of the new RED base after we tracked it down, had to make new web updates, and it was all a frenzy of work for us." Oulaire took a long draw from his long-necked bottle.

"But you wouldn't have had to do any of that work… you're the military general," Tom said.

"I speak for the entirety of the GREEN Agency here." He ran his hand over his quarter-inch-long hair. "And this is only a small part of the damage. Merely residual that made us notice that there was a high amount of activity going on between the two of you lately."

"Don't speak like we're children," Gary said bluntly. "We know that there's been a battle. We've been *in* the majority of them."

"I know that. I simply have to lay out everything before we can get to our proposition," Oulaire said. "And it wouldn't be a wise idea to start an argument with a military general."

I kept my lips shut, no matter how much I wanted to blurt a stream of expletives in this man's face. How could he be so incompetent? We were capable of handling this ourselves.

"You're no government," said the Trenton. He sounded like he was from Britain, but I couldn't be sure. His voice held an American part to it. "I'm sorry if I haven't introduced myself yet. I'm Lewis Trenton of the RED Agency, Board Member 7."

"It's a pleasure," I said, struggling to keep my composure. I bent my head down. The elegant red walls made me a bit nauseous

"Well, yes we are a government," Oulaire said. "We have our own governmental system running through Europe. We're recognized by MI6 as a separate organization of people. We are citizens of different countries, but in a way…"

"You're not a government as we see it," I said. "We are the United States, though we do have posts in other countries, and the RED has power all over the world. You can't say that for yourself." I kept my eyes on my half-empty bottle on the dark-wood table.

"Well, take Broc James for example," Oulaire said. "He was a member of the US Secret Service for over a year. Don't you consider that a governmental position?"

"He was only there on a mission, trying to gather information," Tom said.

Oulaire looked stunned. We had him off guard. I pounced on the opportunity.

"And plus, did he not fake his name and age on that mission? Come on, we're smarter than you think we are," I said with a grin. "And how did he lose his position? Fired."

"Well," Oulaire said, clearly taken aback, "those things may be true. But we are still a large power. We have larger knowledge, more resources, and more cash than both of your operations combined." His hands clenched.

"That may be so, but you don't have any place in trying to intervene."

"That's what we're here for! We need to stop this now!"

"The question is," Trenton said, "which side will you support in the end?"

Oulaire looked grimly thoughtful. "This is not going to change my opinion."

The waiter walked in for the third time. "Do we know what we would like to order?"

I looked around the table and realized that everyone had been paging through their menu but me. I hustled to find a good item to eat. *Buttered pasta, marinara pasta…skip the pasta. I don't want tuna noodles.*

Oulaire was already ordering.

Pizza. With pepperoni and Italian sausage. There we are.

"And what would you like?"

"Twelve-inch pepperoni and sausage pizza, and please grate on Parmesan afterward," I said.

"No problem."

I examined the hue of my bottle in the silence, waiting for the rest of the people at the table to order and for the waiter to slip back into the kitchen.

"So," Bryan said before I could utter a word. "Which will be your agency of choice?"

"We aren't going into that. If you want us to take sides, then you might as well leave as soon as possible."

"Why must you refuse to take sides in an issue that is very much about what side you choose?" said Trenton. He was very intelligent and said many things I agreed with—not something I had expected from someone whom I had probably battled before. He seemed calm and quiet and unlike other RED agents I've encountered. But still, I did not forget what had happened earlier. The percom thing was unnecessary.

"If push comes to shove, yes, we will take a side, but nothing has happened to make us want or need to choose any given opponent in this battle. The GREEN Agency officially deemed it unnecessary if you want to see the papers to prove it."

"We aren't going to do any more negotiations," I said with finality. "I refuse to do anything more if it is all going to be this smoke and mirrors."

Oulier leaned back in his chair, shaking his head. "Why would you call it smoke and mirrors?"

I clenched my teeth. "This isn't straightforward. Nothing is clear. We need you on our side or we're out of the deal. You can't force us to do anything."

"We have more than enough power to force you to negotiate," Oulaire said. His voice was rising in anger.

"You can't take both of us on," said Trenton. "We refuse to negotiate as well. This isn't a matter of treaty signing. We need to take action or nothing."

"We can force the both of you into negotiation."

"And what will happen then?" I said. "We will resist, and if you are as strong as you say, you will destroy us and thus defeat your purpose of peacemaking."

Oulaire was silent.

"I wish it were that easy to solve, but it isn't. It's more complicated than negotiations will handle. If you want to do it that way, go back in time about 60 years." I put the words out like a shotgun.

The waiter came in to a silent room, passing food around to the people who had ordered it.

I wolfed down my food—the sandwich earlier had been my only food in a while, and it wasn't very much. After everyone had completed the meal, the waiter, scratching his left cheek with his right hand, walked in and picked up the plates.

I stood up once the waiter had left, and this caused everyone else on our side to join me in exiting.

"Monsieur Oulaire," Trenton said, "may I have a word with you after the others have left?"

"Certainly," said Oulaire.

I hurried out of the room as quickly as I could. Our group seemed to be in an extra hurry to get away.

"Trenton is going to try to make some sort of dirty deal, I know it," Tom said. "Trying to lasso Oulaire into his little game."

I said nothing, but inwardly I fumed. Tom was right about this one, no denying that.

I leaned against the double door and peered through the tiny window. Trenton was standing close to Oulaire. Trenton reached into his pocket and pulled out a leather wallet.

I turned my head back to the hall. The other three were no longer there. I was the only witness.

"Bribery."

CHAPTER 11:
CONFRONTATIONS,
NEGOTIATIONS

I woke up in our room at the GREEN Agency the next morning and looked out the window. The sun was coming up behind the off-white curtains. Second day in Paris, second day of negotiations. *This is never going to end.*

Tom sat up in his bed. Good thing, too. He had been snoring.

"You know, you snore really loudly."

"Really?" asked Tom, his voice groggy. He sat up in bed, then lifted himself up and out. "Eh, who cares right now? We don't actually have to do anything today."

"Don't be so sure. Oulaire's going to want us to 'negoti-ate'." I mimicked his French accent.

"Yeah, well I'm still suffering from the jetlag. I slept hor-ribly last night." Tom rubbed his forehead with his left hand, leaning his elbow on his knee. "I hate jetlag more than the RED."

"Can't be *that* bad. I slept fine." I sat back on my bed.

"That's because you're Agent 12. What am I?"

"Agent 15."

"Right…hilarious." Tom shook his head. "Anyway. Are you ready to try and convince Oulaire to join out cause?"

"Nope," I said. "I hate negotiations. I'd be better off back in Tallahassee, but…maybe…" I thought, resting my chin on my fist.

"What are you thinking?" Tom said.

"Tom, do you think you could cover me here? Like, could you be the delegate instead of me? I'd be more useful back at the base. I could just go home instead of Bryan to be present at the meeting, and the replacement could stay there at the base."

"I see," Tom said. "I'd take over for you, but why not Gary or Bryan? They'll still be here."

"Neither knows enough to negotiate with these people. You and I are the most knowledgeable of us on the GREEN Agency, and since I need to go back to the base, you should cover for me. It's a good plan, wouldn't you say?"

"Eh, all right," Tom said. "I'd go with that. Not like there's any downside. I was going to be negotiating anyway."

I smiled and picked up my percom. I wouldn't have to negotiate any more and hopefully Oulaire would be fine with me leaving the country.

"Agent D here. Do we have everything in order, Josiah?"

"Almost," I said. "Could we make a change in plans?"

"I'm listening."

"I could come back instead of Bryan, and Tom could cover for me. The replacement would be able to stay in Tallahassee as well. I think it's an all around good idea. Do you see any holes that I'm missing?"

"Aren't you supposed to be the delegate?" she asked.

"I dunno...I'd have to run that by Oulaire. I'll get back to you, but I think Tom will do just fine."

"Does he word things properly? I'm afraid he'll screw things up by throwing an angry rant."

"He'll be able to keep his cool when he's sitting in front of Oulaire. Remember, you feel very small next to this guy."

Silence for a moment.

"Moving on...I got a transcript from Oulaire about the negotiations. Apparently he had the room bugged—you should be careful what you say. But you sounded confident."

"We were having a hard time, don't be fooled. I think we'd better watch out for this Trenton character—seems slimy to me."

"Trenton is one of the best...but he can be very slimy. He should be on our side—I tried to get him to come with me to the BLUE Agency. But Frederick was too strong of an influence. It was almost as if he was enslaved to him."

"And it looks like Trenton has Oulaire wrapped around his little finger...he had a word with him after the meeting, and by the tone of his voice when I left it didn't sound like it was going to be a clean deal he was laying out. Saw him take out his wallet."

Denise was silent. Then, "This will complicate things."

"Do we have any plans for flight?

"I'll handle that for you. I'll get you a direct flight to Tallahassee for two o'clock tomorrow afternoon, private jet, fully furnished with a bed and dining room."

"Thanks, Denise. You're the best."

"You're welcome. Don't expect that every time, though. It'll take me an hour or two to organize this. Every hour we waste is an hour we could have prepared for the next RED attack. Or so says the officer who needs something approved and won't stop bothering me about it. I hope to see you tomorrow, Jones."

The transmission ended with a click.

"Sounded like she went with it…and I agree about the Trenton guy." Tom had dressed in the bathroom while I had talked with Denise.

"We're probably going to be called down for—"

Before I could say another word, my percom beeped to signal someone was calling.

"—breakfast. Right on time." I picked up the percom. "We're coming."

"Good," said Oulaire. "I've made some important changes in opinion," he said quietly. Before I could say a word, the transmission ended.

"Let's go," Tom said.

I slowly hooked my percom to my belt. "He said he'd made some important changes in opinion. Think it has anything to do with his little chat with Trenton?"

"I don't know, we'll find out in a minute. It doesn't matter. We can only hope they have pancakes and bacon."

"Good day, Josiah, Tom, Bryan, Gary," said Oulaire. "Please, sit."

I sat down across from Trenton. He was smiling in a cruel way that didn't make me want to negotiate.

The same mustached waiter walked in from the kitchen.

"Drinks, anyone? We have our morning juices and drinks. What would you like, Monsieur Oulaire?"

"House orange, carbonated, bottled, ice cold, no pulp," he said quickly.

"And you?" The waiter looked at me.

"Same as him," I said.

I looked at the waiter as he asked everyone else for orders. Just then his sleeve button reflected light right into my eye, causing me to turn away. *Oddly shiny sleeve button there.*

The waiter left the room, scratching his mustache with his right arm and mumbling to himself.

"So what are these changes in opinion?" I asked Oulaire.

"I have decided to bring the GREEN Agency military into the situation. We will be guarding both agencies' buildings with our own men. We are prepared to defend both sides if one decides to invade the other, and in this manner we will stop the fighting with defense. It should work, I think?"

Oh, I'm sure THAT will be effective. "You're welcome to do that," I said, "but it won't stop much."

"You have no clue about how large this army is. We have more power, more weapons and technology than both of you combined."

Trenton shook his head. "You have no clue about what the RED Agency has in store for—"

"We actually do. The GREEN Agency has connections everywhere. Even your most secret locations are on camera. We watch your science labs in particular."

"What, then?"

The room was silent.

"Go on. What are we planning?" Trenton waited a few seconds.

"I don't watch the cameras personally—that would be found in the records."

"Find it in there, then," I said.

However, he was saved by the sliding door and the entrance of the waiter, handing out drinks and asking for what we wanted to order.

I cracked open my orange bottle and took a drink...it was atrocious, but I swallowed to keep good image.

"What would you like to have, Monsieur?" said the waiter to me carefully after taking Trenton's and Oulaire's orders.

"Chocolate chip pancakes, five strips of bacon. Nothing on the pancakes. No syrup, no butter," I said.

I looked at his sleeve buttons. They were black with a chrome circle around them—that was why they had glinted.

"Oulaire," I said. "There has been a slight change of plans in who will go back to the BLUE."

"Hm?" Oulaire said.

"Agent D would like me to go back instead of Bryan and have Tom as my replacement delegate," I said.

Oulaire looked thoughtful. "Is Tom qualified?"

"Definitely," I said.

Oulaire nodded. "As long as the delegations continue."

"I would leave tomorrow at one o'clock from this headquarters to the airport," I said.

The waiter swooped in once again with a tray of plates, his face red as if he had run a marathon.

A plate of four large chocolate chip pancakes was set in front of me. Beside it, a small plate covered with more bacon than I had asked for joined the pancakes.

The rest of breakfast was silent—everyone was concentrating on his food, or at least so it appeared. I know that I wasn't focused on breakfast…I was thinking about why it was so important that I would be at the BLUE headquarters instead of keeping the negotiations under control here at the GREEN. Unable to figure this out, my brain switched to the barely-working mode.

I looked at Oulaire, who was cutting into a pile of crepes, topped with strawberries and blueberries. He was giving Trenton shuddering looks every half-minute or so when he wasn't cutting and chewing a large piece of breakfast.

I looked at the position of his chair. It was scooted toward our side of the table. It was almost like…Trenton *makes him nervous.*

I looked at Trenton. He lightly ate his eggs Benedict, chewing slowly on the English muffin and Canadian bacon. It wasn't the food—it was his eyes. Calm, but slightly dark in expression, and aimed toward Oulaire's face.

I can't believe it. Trenton is rather slimy, but not even I am afraid of him. I wonder why he worries Oulaire this much. Either way, this is something I can't ignore—I think we might use this to our advantage.

"What? Jean Claude de Oulaire afraid of Lewis Trenton, and you say that Trenton bribed Oulaire?" Tom said. Lucky everyone in the building didn't hear.

"It's not like it's a bad thing," I said. "We can use that to our advantage. That's why I'm telling you. But I don't know about the bribe thing…"

"Well, it's just…Trenton is…well, small, in comparison to Oulaire. In any case, how do you spin this as a good thing?" he said.

"Aren't we all small in comparison to Oulaire?" I lay back

on my bed, propping my head on a stack of pillows. "We can exploit it to bring him over to the BLUE. He's already afraid of the RED delegate, so it shouldn't be too hard to get him from being 'afraid of RED' to 'on the side of BLUE'. And in the meantime, we can think about the bribery. Perhaps Oulaire tricked Trenton? Or the bribe never went down and Oulaire was sickened by Trenton?"

"Hm," Tom said thoughtfully. "I never thought of it that way."

"That's why I'm the top agent."

I got a call on my percom. It was Agent D.

"What do you need?" I said onto the speaker.

"Are you packed? The flight leaves at two tomorrow and I want you to be prepared," she said. "Are you going to be ready to go, or are you going to be too slow and wait until the very last minute as usual?"

"Don't try to be my parent," I said. "I have everything under my control. The negotiations are going even better than I thought they would. Oulaire is nervous the RED delegate, so we have him almost on our side of the argument already. What do you think?"

"Good job, but right now you need to pack. I can tell that you haven't."

"Don't get your shirt in a knot, Denise. It's not until to-morrow."

"Whatever…" Denise's voice trailed off into nothing, and a moment of silence ensued.

"All right, so I'll be ready to go in plenty of time. And you're right, I haven't packed. I was having an important dis-cussion with Tom."

"How important is 'important'?" she said.

"I was telling him stuff he needed to know about being the negotiator. There's some important information needed, and this guy has some weaknesses we can take advantage of."

"I don't need to be told what to do...I'm perfectly capable," Tom objected. He flung himself onto his bed.

"I have to go...more papers to file about new agents. I hate signing contracts."

"Agreed on that, Black. Over and out."

"Over and out."

The transmission ended, and once again I sat on my bed after I had been pacing back and forth. "What is there to pack, really? I didn't bring a whole lot of stuff."

"Eh, I brought an okay load. Look at my suitcase!" There were clothes and other items strewn over the floor around it.

"Man, you're a pretty disorganized guy."

"Really, it's organized chaos. That's what I try to tell people. And they're like 'Sure...you keep telling yourself that, Tom.'"

I laughed. I liked rooming with Tom.

Dinner—another session of negotiations, my next-to-last at the GREEN Agency. I almost didn't want to leave after the conversation at dinner, but I knew I had to the next day.

"Please, dress finely," Oulaire said over the percom. "We are having a special dinner tonight to give you the best of the GREEN Agency before you leave, Monsieur Jones." He sounded pleasant—perhaps this was going to be fun.

"We didn't bring any fine clothes," I said.

"Don't worry—we are bringing some good clothes up to you tonight so you can have a fine evening at the GREEN Agency," Oulaire replied with a laugh. "I will see you at eight o'clock, then."

At around seven-thirty, there was a knock on our door. We had just gotten back from roaming around the building (with permission, of course)—I was tired and didn't want to open the door to some no-faced GREEN agent.

Tom stepped over and turned the knob. Broc stood there with two hangers of clothes and two bags. He silently handed them to Tom and walked away.

The door closed and Tom tossed me a hanger in my size and shoes in my size. We had each been given light blue dress shirts and black dress pants. They looked uncomfortable. A pair of black leather shoes was in the bag.

"Nice," Tom said. He had already changed into his dress shirt.

"Whatever—I hate dress clothes," I said. "I'm not putting them on until dinner."

Twenty minutes later, I was in the clothes, walking out the door with Tom, Bryan, and Gary, who were all wearing the same thing.

"Sharp clothes, eh?" Bryan said.

"Yeah, and unusually comfortable for dress clothes. They looked like they would be uncomfortable," I said. I felt like I was wearing jeans and a tee. "Well, let's make our way."

CHAPTER 12: LAST STRAW

I was surprised by the dim candlelight. It was the only illumination—candles placed every two feet along the table.

Oulaire was finely dressed indeed—he was wearing a white dress shirt with frills around the cuff. He smiled and waved a hand signaling us to sit.

Trenton was already sitting on the other side of the table, dressed in a light red shirt.

"Tonight we would like to present to you a better dinner than usual. We have, this time, more than our usual waiter and chef—he will be accompanied by six others from our kitchen downstairs," Oulaire said.

We had visited the said kitchen—the cakes were excellent.

"Let's get down to business, then, shall we?" Trenton said.

Oulaire looked at him—for a moment, he betrayed an expression of distaste, but he was able to cover it up quickly. "Yes, that's what we're all here for. You only have two sessions left with us, Jones, so let's make these two count."

"How has Agent D been, Jones?" asked Trenton. I wasn't expecting the comment, so I was very thrown off guard.

"Um…that would seem to be inconsequential…" I had no idea what to say.

"Right."

"I have a question," said Tom. "How is it unclear to the GREEN that the RED has a criminal record?"

"There is no proof. They don't have a criminal record besides your little tussle with them these past months," Oulaire said.

"But they have links with a lot of criminals…their goal is to make sure their want for money and power goes unnoticed, they don't want anyone to see their ties with organized crime." Tom looked at me, then back at Oulaire.

"Where is your proof though?" Oulaire asked. "You have no evidence of RED agents involved in *explicitly* criminal acts."

"It would seem to the normal person that the RED is just a company," Bryan said, "but they've attacked and killed, have agents who are at the top of the Mafia. Clark DeCamos, for example; he's known to be directly involved in seventeen Mafia crimes, including four murders and seven grand thefts."

"Once again, no proof," said Oulaire.

"That's just an example of what the RED Agency has done. It started as a little underground crime syndicate, and grew substantially. Why—how—did they grow like this?" Bryan said. "They wanted to stamp out the BLUE."

"Why on earth did we want to 'stamp out' the BLUE Agency?" asked Trenton. "We already had enough on our hands...what with running operations to make sure that—"

"—that your criminal work was done," Bryan said.

"And you kidnapped me," said Gary. "Along with everyone else in your detention block."

"But that's beside the point. The BLUE has been on to you from the beginning—that's what we're for, to take on the organized crime and other large criminal activists. And that's why you wanted to stop us," Bryan said.

"Well, we were small from the beginning and you kept sending investigators into our small operation, which was completely legal and innocent," Trenton said. "We had to grow stronger and more covert to stop you. After all, for the RED, invention is what—"

"—you use to hurt people," I said.

Once again the waiter walked in to save the conversation from going down a terribly awkward road. Oulaire still did not sound irritable at all, even after the argument most against his liking.

"Please, get me a bottled lime, ice cold, no pulp," he said pleasantly. The waiter nodded.

After everyone had ordered their drinks, Oulaire said, "We must get back to the matter at hand—making peace between you two."

"No," I said. "There's no peacemaking because they need to be stopped. We have already outlined this."

Oulaire did not look shaken at all. "I see. Well, there has to be peace eventually. You have just not come to see it yet. Thus we will simply eat and enjoy company tonight."

How am I supposed to enjoy the company of someone like

Trenton? Oh well...act professional, Josiah, act professional.

"All right, then," I said. I smiled widely as genuine I could make it. The waiter once again hurried in, scratching his cheek.

"Some sort of sore on your face?" I asked. He seemed to be too busy mumbling to himself to notice. He stopped scratching, however, and passed along the six bottles to the correct persons (my own was lime so I could win favor with Oulaire by pretending to have similar tastes).

"So," said Oulaire after the waiter had left the room, "how long have you worked at your agencies?"

I didn't know, so I made up a number. "Six years." This seemed to be correct, because Gary nodded.

"Six," said Gary.

"Eight," Bryan said.

"Five," Tom mumbled quietly. He seemed embarrassed.

"I don't wish to disclose information like this," Trenton said. Predictable.

Oulaire then went into a detailed story about how he had gotten to join the GREEN Agency, including a very interesting piece on his time at the BLUE Agency.

"Well, you see, I was twelve years old at the time—I worked at the BLUE facility in Paris, like I always had. I actually saw to the commission of Broc James going onto the Secret Service. He asked for clearance from the BLUE Agency...said he was a small member and had been asked to retrieve some information. Well, I was part of the small office that cleared this kind of thing, so I cleared him after an hour of research.

"I found out about a week later that he wasn't a member of the BLUE Agency, that he was a member of a different agency. It was then that I resigned from my post to investigate this different group—I found that the GREEN Agency fit my wants and needs for an agency perfectly. Of course, then, I had a bias against the RED Agency, but soon it wore off as I heard more and more about the cause of their fight, I became a bit less opinionated about it. I focused more on trying to get people to join the GREEN Agency…both RED and BLUE alike. It's funny; I actually gave misinformation to one RED agent that caused him to join the BLUE. That was quite an incident."

I leaned in. "Who was this person you convinced to join us?"

"I don't know…" Oulaire said. "It was a few years ago. Two, I'd say. But I know he became a spy or something, close to the BLUE leader. Anyway…"

Oulaire continued his talk of his accomplishments as a GREEN agent—I was no longer paying attention. Who had he gotten over to the BLUE's side? Was it one of their group? Could it possibly be…no, David was never in the RED Agency. I knew that for a fact.

But who was it, then? My food came and went faster than I thought it would. I didn't pay attention to anything until Tom whispered, "Do you think Oulaire will ever stop talking about himself?"

I turned around. "Probably not. They usually don't," I whispered in return. "Listen, are you wondering who he got to our side? I know it was a guy, he said that much. It couldn't have been Denise…who's in her inner circle that just joined on a couple years ago?"

"Umm…" Tom was at a loss for words to whisper. "I don't know, actually. I don't know Denise very well. If anyone knew, it would either be you or Denise herself. But I don't know of any spies in her circle…who do you know of that spies on the RED?"

"No clue." I had been racking my brain with the same question, but nothing seemed to fit.

"Ah well," said Tom. "Inconsequential. We'll find out when we're back at base and this negotiation fiasco is all over. I'm currently troubled about Trenton."

I looked over at Trenton. He had a calm expression on his face, but his gaze flitted from person to person around the table. His eyes fixed for a few seconds on Oulaire, who simply smiled back and continued his mindless blabber.

"Well," said Oulaire with the subtlety of a foghorn, "I have to go back to my office…there are some things I must do there, and you all have permission to go wherever you please within the walls of the GREEN Agency. Please, look around!"

"I'd like to have a word with Mr. Jones, in the kitchen if you please," said Trenton.

I looked at him. "All right…" I followed him through the door into the kitchen. Oulaire didn't seem to notice anything at all, while the other BLUE agents seemed puzzled.

"So," said Trenton quietly as we walked into the kitchen, "you do know that you have someone else against you here?"

"What?"

"There is a traitor—one you see frequently during nego-tiations—someone who is right next to you. He wants to hurt you…very much."

"Tom?" I said. "Oulaire?"

"This is all I needed to tell you." His biting voice cut like a knife. "Good night—go, roam around with your friends."

I hurried out of the room, out of the dining room, into

the hall where Tom, Gary, and Bryan awaited me.

"What did he want?" said Tom.

"Umm…" I was hesitant. "Whatever he said, a beaver could have told me better."

After roaming for a couple of hours, I decided that it was time to turn in to bed. I didn't go to sleep for a long time, wondering if Tom would betray me and what in the world Trenton had meant by what he'd said.

Breakfast the next morning was less formal; I simply threw on a t-shirt, jeans, and jacket, and headed to the dining room.

I sat once again next to Tom. I felt uneasy—I still didn't know what Trenton had meant. I tried to shirk it off and think that it was someone else—probably Oulaire. Yes, it must be Oulaire. He seems to be that kind of guy.

Oulaire was in a bad mood. He waved his hand carelessly instead of the welcoming gesture he had made last night. He looked like he was tired—must have stayed up late last night—and didn't want to talk a lot.

Trenton just sat there, smiling like a shark.

"Well," I said, "thank you for having me, Jean Claude. It has been a good time getting to know you and the GREEN Agency," I said.

"That is good," said Oulaire. If he had been annoyed before, there was no sign of it now. "I am glad we were able to host you."

I smiled and nodded.

The kitchen door opened—the waiter was facing sideways, still scratching his face and mumbling. He realized that the door had opened and hustled into the dining room, haphazardly passing around menus.

"Orange," I said before he had given Trenton his menu. I liked seeing the waiter feeling busy and rushed—it was rather comical and cheered me quite quickly.

The waiter muttered something under his breath. I chuckled.

"I wonder why he's always in such a rush," said Tom. I laughed.

"He's busy with food—it looks like he works two jobs. Perhaps he doesn't have a car?" I wondered.

Breakfast was only pleasant conversation. I was glad—I hated having to decide whether to trust Tom or not. Trenton spent most of his time talking with Oulaire in a tense voice.

I, however, spent my time talking to Tom.

"How do you feel about being left here?" I asked.

"Eh…" Tom's eyes glazed over. "It isn't that bad. I mean, Oulaire's kind enough to let us stay here with pretty good rooms. And the food is great."

"Do you think the BLUE will still pay you for this?" I grinned.

Tom chuckled. "I dunno…maybe. I wouldn't put it past them to not pay me, what with everything being expensive. And it's not like I would miss it."

"So it's not about the money for you?"

"What, it is for you?" Tom laughed. "It's all about the adventures and excitement. We get to use all this cool equipment before the US army does. It's like being a superhero, except you can't be caught for vigilantism or have your girlfriend stolen for it."

"Good point," I said. The conversation lulled as I chewed a little of my waffle. "Hey, have you heard anything about

Gary and Denise? Now that he's alive…"

"Don't go into that," Tom said with a scoff. "Denise probably won't go for him. If so, it'd be very…*weird.*"

"I was just joking, you know…jokes? The funny things that, when employed in conversation, help keep the ice broken."

"Denise only found out less than a week ago that Gary was even alive. I don't see that as very good dating prospects."

I looked around the table. "I'm glad to get out of here today."

"Why?" Tom said. "It's not that bad, 'cept the negotiation part."

"That's my point. I hate negotiating, and I hate spending time around Trenton."

"Why so? He isn't that bad."

I gulped and wondered for a second if I should confide in him what he had said the night before. "Umm…can you keep this to yourself?"

"What?"

"Last night, when Trenton wanted to talk, he said that there was someone out to get me that I was next to every day, during negotiations."

"What? No way…Oulaire isn't dangerous."

"I…I don't think he meant Oulaire," I said, stuttering.

"Who—oh, I get it. You thought he meant me?"

"Yeah," I said slowly. "I don't think you're a traitor though. Don't get me wrong. You're a great guy. But why would he say that?"

Tom looked disturbed. "No clue. Perhaps a scare tactic?"

I surveyed Trenton. His head was turned to face Oulaire, Trenton's thin lips barely moving as he talked tensely.

"Yes, definitely a scare tactic." I was glad to be able to justify pushing the thought of Tom being a traitor out of my mind.

"Just take Trenton off your mind. After all, he *is* a RED agent. They tend to be slippery."

Even though I said I was ready to leave the RED headquarters, I never imagined that I would feel this way leaving it.

Or rather, leaving Tom, Bryan, and Gary to fend for themselves in this crazy negotiation thing the GREEN was trying to pull off.

Someone rapped at the door. I swung my backpack over my back and rolled my luggage behind me. I opened the door to Broc.

"Are you ready?" he said. "Do you need to say goodbye or anything else?"

"No. Tom and the others are at lunch. Let's get this train wreck rolling."

CHAPTER 13: HEADING HOME

The small private jet was waiting for me. It was completely blue, except for two large white circular spots on the side. It was supposed to be a secret reference to the BLUE Agency logo, which contains a large blue circle with two circles side by side cut out of the center. They call it the "double eagle" for reasons no one cares about.

The stairs upward were unmanned: no massive lines walked up the ramp like they had in New York and Paris. This airport was quiet—the Blue Foundation Paris Private Airport, another reference to the BLUE.

I stepped up onto the plane to see a few seats, then a door, through which I walked inside to find that there were three separate rooms through which you could enter. I walked into the one that had a Post-It note on it saying, *"Agent 12's Room,"* assuming that I was the Agent 12 that they were talking about.

It was more spacious than the plane looked like it could hold from the outside. It held a full bed, a dresser, and a pair of armchairs in one corner that had between them a tall stand-up lamp that looked like it was made for reading—all anchored to the floor. It was almost as if I were already back at the BLUE Agency. On the opposite end of the room was a door—it looked like it led to another room. I stepped inside to see what was there.

A table and chairs adorned the center. At the table sat two people whom I knew very well.

"Hey, Josiah!" David said with a smile. He stood up and shook my hand vigorously.

The other person followed his example. KC. "Good to see you again, Josiah," she said in a professional tone.

"What are you two fools doing on here?" I grinned widely, happy to see that they had sent people I knew to accompany me back home. *Man, I have things to tell people when we get back in Tallahassee. Most people probably still don't know about the GREEN Agency yet.* "Did you guys hear about the GREEN Agency? Or rather, has the rest of the entire BLUE heard about the GREEN?"

"We have, but Denise has been so busy working with a whole bunch of new submissions to the agency that she hasn't been able to send out a memo or anything. We've been trying to recover some of the losses we've made in previous battles. Add that to our normal selection enrollment you get one tired Denise," David said.

"That's what she was complaining about on the percom?"

"Probably." David smiled. "She's quite open to you, isn't

she? Come on, Josiah—sit down. It's a long plane ride."

I sat in a chair next to David.

"So what is the GREEN Agency like?" he said.

"We're preparing for takeoff. Please buckle up," said the captain.

I reached for a seat belt, but only found a buckle hanging as if strung with invisible thread to the seat.

"Just buckle it. You don't feel anything unless it really needs to restrain you," said KC.

"The GREEN Agency is nothing terrible and nothing exciting, really. We spent most of our time in our rooms or in the dining room for negotiations. They did have some awesome meals, though. And the lobby is the most beautiful room you'll ever see."

"How did the negotiations go? Were you convincing?" KC asked.

"It wasn't the kind of negotiations where we were trying to win them to our side. At least they weren't supposed to be. That's what it turned into though. We were both trying to get the GREEN to our side."

"What help would that be? If we've never heard of them, they can't be that big," David said.

"Not so...GREEN is just a recent alias. I don't know what they're truly called, but by the way they put it, this isn't the first name they've had. Who knows? We've probably dealt with them in the past and haven't known about it." I sighed and rubbed my forehead. The plane was going at an incline, making my ears pop.

"It sounds complicated," he said. "Now what about this Lewis Trenton person we keep hearing about?"

I rolled my eyes. "He's bad news. Slimy, cheating, and

tries to use scare tactics."

"Give an example," she said.

"That's like asking when water is wet. He's always making sure he gets to meals before us so he can convince Oulaire a bit more. We thought for a while that Oulaire was afraid of Trenton, but he isn't showing it lately. And Trenton pulls Oulaire over sometimes to convince him more. And he told me that I was next to a traitor every day at meals—I think he meant Tom." I breathed again.

"He doesn't sound like Mr. Nice Guy," said KC.

"No kidding." I rubbed my forehead again. The plane leveled out in the air. "So, what's been going on? Anything else happened at home while I was gone?"

"We figured out where the new RED base is," KC said. "You and Tom helped us a little bit—we had your car bugged."

"How did you know we were leaving?" I said, astonished.

"We didn't. We just have them bugged anyway." David smiled slyly.

I laughed. "Why don't I know these things?"

"It's all in the little white book. All BLUE cars are usually bugged so we can know if something's been stolen and so we can make sure we have no...deviators, if you know what I mean." David leaned back, his glasses glinting from the light on the ceiling.

"Yeah, I think I get what you mean," I said.

"We actually thought you guys were leaving the BLUE Agency for good when you left that night. Good thing we found out that you were just after Gary. Otherwise, there would have been so much of a mess. You probably would have been fired and arrested at the same time...." KC said.

"Oh, stop, KC," David said. "She's just messing with you. You would have been messaged beforehand if we were going to come for you."

"So, you know where the RED base is now. What about it?" I asked.

"We're currently planning to launch an infiltration on the building using the information you were provided on the website. We found it to be very useful to us. After we have everything perfect, we can have people in RED uniforms infiltrate quite easily. The rest is to be discussed at the meeting that will now take place tomorrow." David took off his sunglasses, revealing his dark eyes.

"Isn't that too risky, so soon after we got caught doing the same thing?" I said. "Don't you think there's another way?"

"We're not necessarily taking the offensive here, just going to get some information, like last time. At least, that's what's proposed."

"That's what's 'proposed,'" I repeated to David. "Proposed doesn't mean that's what's going to happen. Propositions or not, it's an all around bad idea. Shouldn't we gear up for another one of their attacks?"

"We're trying to do that too, but Agent D said that's a bit of a conflict of interests," David replied.

"She says we'd stretch ourselves too thin," KC added.

"Do we spend more time and effort on gearing up or on getting ready to attack? I'm for the preparation for being attacked," David continued without acknowledging KC. "I don't think we'll get anywhere trying to take the offensive. The RED Agency would hear about it...and they wouldn't be happy."

"Agreed," I said.

"Attack *could* work," KC said.

"But what of the negotiations? What if those don't go over well and the GREEN decides to join with the RED Agency? Look at it from every angle and all I see is a victory for the RED," David said.

I sighed and shook my head slowly. "Maybe the GREEN is right. We might need to solve this via peace negotiations."

David managed a heartless laugh. "The RED won't co-operate with that, let me tell you right now. Especially with a representative like Lewis Trenton. He can tackle anyone in a war of words."

I sighed again. This was tiring.

"I'm going to my room to read," said David. He walked to his room, and KC did the same thing, slowly standing up and walking into her room.

After twirling around in my chair for a few seconds, I stepped into my room and crashed onto the bed, facedown.

I turned over after awhile, my face sweaty from having it lie on the thick pillow. Scooting back, I opened my bag and, for the first time on this trip, I pulled out my e-j. I wrote:

"Why does everything have to be so complicated in the imaginary world? I guess it's better than taking end-of-the-year tests at home...

"My birthday is coming up soon. I get to celebrate my birthday twice this year. That's something cool about living in the imaginary world. I hope the RED doesn't attack on my birthday. That would suck pretty badly.

"I hope Denise is doing okay at HQ...and I hope Tom is able to hold up during the negotiations."

Feeling too tired to press the pen to the screen, I turned off my e-j and closed my eyes.

"Agent 12! Get up and get a weapon! There's an ambush waiting for us as soon as we land!"

My eyes were open now, hazy...there was David...he was shaking my shoulder....

"Josiah! They're going to destroy the plane!"

CHAPTER 14: BACK AT BASE

I sat up instantly, alert and ready for action.

"What's going on?"

"At the airport—they sent a distress signal. Ambush. They're waiting for us and will attack once we exit the plane. Get your stuff!"

I opened my suitcase and took out the prototype B5, armor, and a carbonyssium carbine.

"We've got to move." I followed him out of my room through the cabin—KC was already waiting by the exit. "We're landing in five minutes and this plane has very limited battle capabilities—only two guns with a magazine each loaded near the front. We don't think we can aim with those, but…"

David kept giving instructions as I threw on armor and waited for the landing signal outside the exit.

I held my gun, my hand shaking. David had stopped giving the situation—all I knew was that it was time to fight. My hand was sweaty and slippery now.

"Do you guys have any shields?" I asked nervously. *Calm down…it can't be much worse than at the RED detention floor….*

"We have ours on," David said. "You don't?"

I was quick to think and ran back to my room. I hurried through my suitcase and finally found the shield unit, slipping it over my arm.

I returned, heaving fast breaths, to the door.

"Relax," David said. "And keep your cool. No need waste your energy on shaking. Got it?"

I breathed in slowly. That helped. The blood pumped slower with every beat of my heart. I began to relax.

"Aren't you a bit freaked out?" KC asked David shakily.

"Just get ready. Calm down, both of you. Don't sweat it."

I felt the digestion slowing in my stomach as adrenaline began to return to my body. We were coming in for a landing.

The plane touched down with a skid of the wheels.

Excitement rushed. The plane slowed finally to a stop.

The door swung open. I threw the B5 at the ground. It caught itself, hovering, before it hit the ground. I jumped onto the platform and leaned forward. I was speeding ahead, going faster than both of the others even though they ran at full speed. I brandished the stun laser. *Don't be too harsh—we can't kill these people. We might need them for interrogation later.*

The RED agents came speeding out of the hangar—literally! The spearhead of four agents shot out on motorcycles equipped with weaponry.

I sped faster toward them, but could only go so fast. *We've gotta put some more speed on this thing before the next prototype can be released.*

But with no more time to think, bolts of energy came at me from the motorcycles. I swerved around the bikes—the B5's force pushed one of the cyclists off, but he landed on the ground, his motorcycle spinning and skidding to a stop.

The heat of their blasts caused me to start sweating—the shield didn't block heat, but the coolant in my armor quickly cooled me. I squeezed the trigger at the group of about fifteen agents behind the motorcycling ones. Missed one—only by inches, though.

A couple of the cyclists came around. No one was focusing on David and KC—why?

I swerved as another one of the cyclists came barreling toward me. Simultaneously, I fired three shots straight at three RED agents, blasting them onto the hangar wall, but not knocking them unconscious.

I wonder...what? Do they have shields? And how are they not overloading?

A couple of them were down, but they weren't overloaded either. And the shots didn't disappear away from the body like on a normal shield. They kind of were absorbed into the suits they were wearing. *They must have some kind of armor that absorbs the energy. That means we have to shoot in places where the only thing protecting them is the cloth.*

"Avoid shooting the armor! It's energy-absorbing! Aim for the black!" I shouted at the very top of my already-strained lungs. I fired quickly at an area of black cloth. The agent was down and stunned instantly.

KC and David followed suit. The RED agents didn't

stand a chance.

I felt something bump harshly. I was swerving to the side: a stray shot had hit my unshielded B5.

I continued to fire, but the Braulter jolted me nearly off of it. Thinking quickly, I pressed the power button with my left (non-shooting) hand. Unfortunately, I had just jumped a tire from a motorcycle, leaving me to fall ten feet to the ground attached to a powered-off vehicle.

I kicked hard to the back, launching the B5 backwards. It hit the plane, denting the side of the B5 quite a bit.

I bent and rolled instantly after the landing. Jumping lessons had served me well.

Pulling myself to my feet, I fired hard. These were the people who had taken Gary. They had stolen from people, murdered, oppressed. And the world, not knowing it was these people, had felt it.

The cyclists soon abandoned their vehicles once they had become too broken to drive anymore—four red motorcycles now were strewn across the airport, and twenty half-awake RED agents lay, disarmed, against the hangar wall.

"We need to get these RED agents back to headquarters," David said smoothly.

"I'll call Denise. KC, you'd better go into the hangar to see what's going on in there. Be ready with your weapon. There may be more RED agents," I said.

"Will do." KC hurried off the runway into the hangar. She slowed down as she entered the building.

The plane's door burst open, and the pilot, co-pilot, and flight attendant nearly jumped the staircase. "Good job, guys! Well done!" the pilot said. "We were afraid for your life, Jones. They were probably after you."

"But how did they know about this flight?" I said.

"The RED delegate must have leaked something back to base. There's no other way they could have known," David said, meandering toward the airplane personnel.

KC came out of the building confidently, and behind her came the airport security and several thankful BLUE agents.

"Good work, KC. Were there any more REDs inside?" I said.

"Negative. They were just being safe and didn't come out. It was a smart move—I'd hate for innocent agents to be caught in our crossfire." KC was back at the scene of the battle now, and the pilot was shaking hands with the security guards.

"Well, they could have helped out a bit. Especially you, Agent 5." I pointed to an agent from my own regiment who stood among the airport staff.

"Sorry, just my orders, sir," said Agent 5.

"Don't worry about it," David said. "Right now you need to call Agent D, 12."

"Right." I picked up my percom and dialed for Agent D.

"I heard that there was going to be an ambush at the airport. Did you handle it well?" Agent D said quickly.

"Yes, no casualties on our side except for the B5. It would help if you could bring over some cars to put these RED agents in. We need to keep them for some interrogation. Or we can release them back if you want to…"

"No, I'll send some people. How many do you have stunned?"

"Twenty."

"We'll send some people to pick them up. But don't worry about that right now—you need to get back here in time for the meeting. Remember?"

I hadn't remembered. "Who's going to be there?"

"You'll find out when you get there. David's car is next to the hanger. You have my permission to come back to base."

"Got you. Over and out."

I clicked the button to hang up. "Let's go," I said. "Denise is sending some people to take care of the rest. You guys can go back to work." I pointed at the hangar staff.

"I'm driving," David said.

"Shotgun," I said.

"Good to have you back," Denise said. She was sitting at her computer. Her chair turned around quickly. Her face looked tired, bags under her eyes and what seemed to be a small wince glued to her face.

"You were afraid I was going to get killed in that little fiasco over at the airport?" I laughed. "You know me better than that."

"We don't have time to talk about that. Let's get to conference room A."

Steve, KC, David, and several other agents were seated and talking impatiently. Denise and I sat at the ends of the long, metal-topped table.

"All right, let's get some order here," Denise said. "Please welcome back our straight-from-Paris agent, Josiah Jones."

Several agents clapped, and the entire room broke into a short applause. I smiled. "As long as I'm not in any trouble..."

"We have some new updates to share that will complicate things a little bit. As you know, we have discovered that there is an agency called the GREEN, and they are attempting to have a negotiation with the BLUE and the RED agencies."

"What?" Steve said. "Why are they expecting the RED to cooperate with a negotiation?"

"This is exactly why we must change the topic of the negotiations from trying to stop the conflict to persuading the GREEN's forces to come to our own side," I said. "The RED Agency wants the same thing, so we have to convince the GREEN to come to our side before the RED's grimy hands get a hold on the GREEN."

"But that's all up to Tom of PRLO," Denise said. "What we really need to talk about as of right now is whether we will attack or defend. Thoughts?"

After a short period of silence, David said, "I say we need to defend our base at all costs." He pounded his fist on the table, shaking my blue notebook and pen. "We have everything to lose here. We have no backup for this base. I know that it was an error, but it's still a fact."

"What? What's the point in defending?" said another agent—one I didn't know very well, but I knew to be an All-Force agent. "It's time to stop playing around—the RED aren't. If we attack, we have *nothing* to lose."

"Oh yes we do," I said. "If we do an infiltration squad, it would take our best agents including me. That would also leave us vulnerable to any attack the RED makes. Beside the fact that two of the best agents have already failed to get in there without being chucked into a prison cell. Not meaning to be cocky or anything, but..."

The room erupted into pandemonium. People shouted at each other with angry comments and inflamed responses.

"Quiet!" Denise bellowed. The room went silent. "I am personally on the side of taking the defensive. All agreed, say

'I.'"

"I," said about half the people in attendance. I saw five people say the word.

"All opposed?"

Four people said "I."

"It's six to four. In the democratic sense, we should go on with defending, but are there some other ideas?"

"We absolutely have to gear up for both!" Steve said, who had not said "I" to either statement.

"Explain."

"We can't attack and leave our base vulnerable, but we can't pull into a turtle shell and wait for something to happen. Neither would be helpful, only hurtful to our cause." Steve leaned forward.

"I agree, but that's stretching us too thin," Denise said. "We only have so much time and about as many resources for assault as a pig farmer. Yes, it would be nice if we could, but right now, that isn't an option unless we have the GREEN on our side."

Steve was silent for a long moment. "Then I take my side on defense," he said with finality, and leaned back in his chair. Every terrified pair of eyes was on Steve.

"We vote once again. All in favor of defense?"

"I." Every voice in the room backed this one.

"All opposed?"

Sweet silence.

"All right. We'll double our efforts to defend the BLUE main headquarters here in Tallahassee." Denise smiled widely and looked at me, then Steve. We started clapping.

The room burst into applause.

CHAPTER 15: HUNCHES

My office felt more natural to me than usual. With over a week of absence, the place was more like a home than it ever was.

The door slid open. I swiveled around: it was Steve, who wore a broad smile. It was the first time I had seen that face in a long time. I stood to greet him.

"Hey, Steve!" I said. "You did a good job convincing the rest of the meeting back there. You made everything a whole lot shorter."

"Thanks," Steve said. "I wasn't aiming to do that, but you're welcome anyway. I was just saying that I'm sorry for exploding at you verbally a couple months ago. I was just angry. But now that you saved Gary…"

"You have Broc James to thank for that," I said. "He was the one who broke us out."

"Really?" Steve said. "I did a database file recently on him.

He and I were close friends."

"When?"

"In his Secret Service year. I was one of the few people who actually knew that he wasn't who he said he was." Steve smiled.

"He looks like he could be my age. How did he—"

"Prosthetics and a lot of makeup. He did a good job, too."

"That's good to hear," I said. "So…do you have any other updates for me on the Braulter?"

"Why do you keep calling it that? It's been renamed to B5. Anyway, we've been designing the second prototype. I decided to add a shield to this one—bet you're happy about that, especially after the last one's death. It's not a good idea to use prototypes in the field."

"*That* was Tom's idea to bring. I'm surprised we didn't get in trouble for the fiasco that we caused. Agent D must be lenient of late. And by the way, the B5 definitely needs more speed," I said with a smirk. I motioned for Steve to sit down in the white armchair beside my desk.

"Well, yes, she is being lenient, but it's probably because you were doing something important enough to let you off the hook, considering the GREEN would be our only hope to take down the RED. Plus you're one of the top agents, and so is Tom, so getting you guys in trouble would set a bad mood for in the agency, and we can't have that happen."

"Well, what's the point of our battles at this time?" I said. "Why are we even fighting?"

"It's mostly on their part revenge, on our part defense," Steve said. "But it's a complicated revenge, because once they get it they aren't done. They want to go to a full-scale change of public thinking that is against everything we stand for. That's why they want political power, and that's why we're trying to stop them. And of course, we want to keep agents like you intact."

Leaning my chin on my hand, I said, "I never understood exactly what the RED wants."

"All you can understand now is that whatever it is, it's not good. No one in the BLUE Agency knows *exactly*, but there are a lot of hunches."

"What's your idea?"

"I, uh…" Steve scratched his scalp. "I think it's more of a fight for them to be able to do whatever they want without interference."

"What exactly would they want to do?"

"Nothing as simple as 'ruling the world.' More like, being able to get their ideas made into authority. What they want is to trump the law."

"But that's what I'm looking for: what are their ideals?"

Steve sat silently for a few seconds. "That's hard to pin down, Josiah. I can't think of anything right now."

A percom beeped and I reached to pick it up.

"That's mine," Steve said. "I have to go," he said after looking at the caller ID. He rushed out of the room fairly quickly.

I sighed and moved back over behind the computer and began to write in my electronic journal about the meeting and everything Steve and I had just talked about. It was then that I received a message on my percom.

It was Agent D. "Hey, Denise. What do you need?"

"I actually finished all the application papers. Apparently I was going so fast that I got them done faster than I would have because of the fact there were so many."

"Don't exactly get how that works, but cool," I said. "What does that mean?"

"Do you, David, and Bob want to watch a movie?"

"Sure. In the Seclab?"

"Yep. Meet me in five. I already sent the other two messages."

"But why isn't KC coming? I'm sure she'd like to."

"She said she was busy with something...and she couldn't tell me what it was. I tried to force her, but...oh well."

"I'll see you in five minutes."

I hung up and walked out the door. *KC has been rather mysterious lately. I hope she's all right.*

"So, what did you really call us down here for?" Bob asked warily. He eyed Denise.

"To watch a movie," Denise said plainly. "What do you want to see?"

"I think you're hiding something. What is it you need to talk about?" Bob said. "It seems unrealistic that..."

"Don't turn into another conspiracy theorist," David said with a laugh. "We get enough of that from Tom."

I laughed, even though I knew Tom better than that now. "Hey, it's good to see you again, Bob. I'm glad to be back at the headquarters."

"You too, Josiah. I don't know what to watch—is there a specific movie that you had in mind?"

"I dunno...*The Lion King*," Denise said.

"Good movie. Let's watch it," I said. "Put it in...in the meantime, I'll make some food."

Two bags of microwave popcorn, a frozen pizza, and three sodas later, we had stopped watching the movie and were instead sitting on the couch and chairs. I claimed the couch for myself and stretched my legs.

"Denise, quick question," Bob said. "How exactly are we gearing up for defense right now?"

"Um…" Denise shifted and looked over to David for support. He simply nodded. "Currently we're working on upping security around entrances and building a larger shield around the entire base. We've been working on the shield for a few years now, trying to perfect it. Now we're going to have to go with what we already have."

"And what else?" David said. He wore a frown now, sipping a blue soda.

"We're working on beefing up the armor, and the release of the new shields has been a tremendous help. Plus registration was a total success and the reason for my tiredness, as well as placing some lower-level agents in positions as trainers part-time so they can be active duty and bring up new agents strong along the way."

"New armor?" My ears perked up at the idea. I had been growing tired of the same armor suits (they were uncomfortable in the knees). We needed improvement.

"Yes. But one of the prototypes was stolen by the RED Agency a couple of months ago. That's what you saw in the battle: the absorbent armor. But we've improved on it since then; at least the cloth will protect a bit more. It's all we could do—we have no time to develop energy-absorbent cloth."

I swirled the soda in my can. "What else?"

"We have also expedited the B5's production. We're going to be working more hours to get that done, because really it's a great idea. And I mean it when I say that."

"Thanks," I said. "That's what I was thinking."

"The rest relies on Tom, Bryan, and Gary to get the GREEN on our side." David looked more at ease now. The frown had dissipated and was replaced by his normal, expressionless face.

"I hate doing the paperwork involved in our kind of war. I wish it would be over; that would make my job a heck of a lot easier," Denise said. She breathed in deeply.

"I agree," I said, "but we have to keep going. If we give up now you won't have a job at all."

"Maybe it would just be better not to work here then," Denise said.

Bob laughed. "Josiah's right, though—we won't have much of a life at all if we give up and leave the BLUE. The RED Agency would take over, and then what would become of us?"

Denise was silent. "I don't know, but I don't want to think about it."

Night came on. I was lying in my bed, looking up at the ceiling. "I wish I could see the stars," I said. I hadn't seen anything natural for a while, besides outside the airport and in the lobby in Paris.

"Commence Stars program?" said the computer.

We have voice activation? "What? Stars program?"

"The Stars program gives you realistic environments based on what is outside in the sky. Do you wish to run this application?"

"Yes," I said.

The ceiling faded into black, and dots of light sparkled on it. It looked just like did outside.

I breathed in deeply and went to sleep, the faint light of

the moon shining on my face for the first time in months.

Two days passed quickly. Steve made a new (and large) entry in the database for the GREEN Agency; this caused many people to become confused. Denise announced the entire situation and everyone went berserk with questions.

And, of course, the majority of those questions were directed to me.

"Agent Jones, what is the GREEN Agency?" "Agent 12, can you give us some more info on the newly discovered GREEN group?" "What's going on with the negotiations?"

I could hardly move without being asked about the GREEN Agency. Even sitting down to eat a sandwich at lunch, I was bombarded with questions. I felt bogged down and went to my room to get some rest.

It felt so peaceful—looking up at the midday sky. There were a few cumulus clouds here and there, but it was mostly a deep, rich and wonderful navy color, a quarter-sized circle of light representing the sun.

I watched the clouds move. It was an amazing simulation.

Tearing my gaze from the ceiling, I sat down at my white desk and logged into my computer. I wrote in my e-j:

"The Stars application is so beautiful...I wonder who designed it. I'll ask Steve, but it's stunning. A great thing to help you relax when you know that the RED Agency could attack at any moment."

I dialed Steve's code into my percom.

"Hey, Steve...are you familiar with the Stars application?"

"Definitely," he replied. "I designed it."

I paused for a moment. "Cool. And I didn't know that I had voice activation. How did that happen?"

Steve laughed. "You've had it for years...you must have accidentally clicked the icon on your computer. I thought you knew about that."

"No, I didn't. Lemme guess—it was in the little white book. The application, though—great simulation! It's quite relaxing."

"Hey, I gotta go...have to work on the B5 prototype. Should be done with that tomorrow, so I'm going to show that to you. Catch you later."

Steve hung up. *I'd better go to the gym—I haven't had a workout in a while, I thought to myself.*

The walk to the gym made me think about Tom, Gary, and Bryan in Paris. *I wonder...what are they talking about right now? Maybe I should give them a call when I get on the treadmill.*

In the gym, I saw that there were only two other people: Bob and KC. I smiled and ran up to the treadmills, standing on the one between them.

"Hey, guys," I said. I wore a smile on my face.

"'Sup, Jo?" Bob said. "Do you mind if I call you Jo?"

"Not at all." He was the second person ever to ask me that. *He and Tom...they seem quite similar.*

KC just kept running. Her meter said she'd been running for ten minutes, yet she hadn't even broken a sweat. She was going at a steady 8 miles per hour, no less.

I looked over at her. She had a somber look glued to her face as if she hadn't put it there.

"Hey, why weren't you hanging with the rest of us in the Seclab?" I asked.

"I said to Denise that I was busy, and I meant it." KC sounded annoyed, and grimaced as she turned up the speed.

"I'd better call Tom," I said. "He's probably having a rough time with the negotiations, and he needs all the encouragement he can get considering the fate of the BLUE Agency is resting on his shoulders."

"Yeah, and you're the one who's being hammered with questions about the GREEN Agency," KC said with a small laugh.

"Thanks," I said flatly. I pushed the buttons to start the treadmill, beginning at two miles an hour. I dialed Tom.

"Hey, Josiah. What's up? Do we have any news?" Tom said.

"Some good news," I said. "Well—there's a little bit of bad mixed in, but we're mostly doing a-okay. How are the negotiations?"

"Slow," Tom said. I put the percom on speakerphone and put it in the slot on the treadmill. "Jean Claude de Oulaire is pretty stubborn, no matter how he masks himself to be kind. He also doesn't take 'no' for an answer."

"We figured that much," I said.

"Yeah, well, Trenton has been encountering the same trouble. Or so he said to me after a meeting. I wonder why he told me that…"

"He's very intelligent. Too intelligent to tell someone on the opposite side he's having trouble," I said. "And we often agree on many things. It's just we disagree on one big thing: morals or power."

I could almost see Tom's dismal expression.

"So, that's about it. It's going slow and there's not much to report. Oulaire isn't showing that he's afraid of Trenton, so that hope's gone. Anyway, I'm going to let you go. I have to eat something."

"Bye, Tom."

The line disconnected.

"Doesn't sound like it'll be an easy battle right now," KC said, shaking her head. "We need to get our heads in the game and work."

"What do you mean?"

"What can this de Oulaire guy do to stop us?" she said confidently. She upped her speed two-tenths of a mile.

"What makes you think that?" I said. "You've never seen Jean Claude de Oulaire. He's huge, to say the least; trust me when I say that was an understatement."

"Really?" KC looked dumbfounded. "I thought of him as a short French guy with the curly mustache. But appearances have nothing to do with this."

"Talk about stereotypes..." Bob remarked.

"It was just the first thing that popped into my head when I heard the name. But still, he's not our enemy, is he?"

"He could soon be," I said gravely. "The RED Agency might win him over, and that's the last thing we want to happen. We can't afford to give the RED a the leathal weapon of the GREEN Agency and simultaneously lose out hope of assaulting their base."

All of a sudden, I felt a lurch in my stomach. What was that sound?

I turned off my treadmill and pocketed my percom.

The alarm was blaring. The RED Agency had made their first move.

CHAPTER 16: ONE STRAY SHOT

Bob was the first to rush to the gym's emergency armory. He tossed some light armor and carbonyssium carbines to each of us.

"Come on! Let's move!" I shouted, pulling the front and back plate over my head. I slipped into my helmet and holstered a pistol as extra ammo. "Bob! Shields!"

Three shields were distributed and clicked on. I rushed out of the gym, closely followed by Bob and KC. The barely visible blue bubble of energy hovered less than an inch around my body.

"*All-Force agents, please report to the lobby. We are under attack. Anyone else, remain in the safety of your office and keep armed,*" came a message. I recognized the altered voice of Denise over my helmet percom.

Coolant rushed over my body—at least, the part that was

covered with my suit. My arms were still covered in sweat.

I started to get the signal of one of the generals marshaling the All-Force agents as they streamed inside. He called me to the left side of the wide lobby. I ducked as shots were fired. I felt the heat rush over my body and the coolant responding, flowing ever faster.

The RED agents were running back and forth along the lobby. "What do they want?" I yelled to the general.

"They must be using a scare tactic." The general sounded confident. "Keep firing at the ones you can."

The RED agents streamed in at no more than twenty or thirty at a time, but it was a constant flow. I wondered what the deal was—they could definitely have more guys in the lobby.

Amid the sound of the shots, I heard the general yell, "There's no way to get them down! Their armor is staying intact!"

I knew what was happening. "General! Tell them to shoot for the unarmored areas. That'll get 'em down!"

"Thanks, Jones! Aim for the Kevlar!"

As soon as everyone knew how to get them down, people started to shoot for the unarmored areas.

One by one, the RED agents fell to the ground, stunned. We had no shield blowouts ourselves, a definite plus. And yet more RED agents advanced, and the number of opponents stayed the same. I fired back, running back and forth and rolling across the floor to avoid shots.

All of a sudden, Denise came barreling out of one of the halls and jumped near the front of the lines. She was wearing the new armor, but no shield.

"Denise!" I shouted. She was fighting vigorously, even with as little protection as she had.

"I'll be fine. You keep fighting!" she said back to me.

"Stay toward the back!" My shouts were drowned out by the morale of the fighting, however. The streams of RED agents kept replenishing themselves over and over—their numbers were increasing now.

She stepped forward, in front of everyone else to hit three RED agents. "Denise, get back!" I shouted, rushing to the front lines.

Perhaps she didn't hear me.

"Percom, reach Agent D," I said. "Denise! Stop! Get back! You must stay behind the front lines!"

I ran to Denise so fast, but I was in no time to protect her. A single blast from a single RED agent hit Denise in the arm, where she was unprotected. She flew back, her gun flying out of her hand. I had felt the heat of the shot as well, and small drops of blood landed on my armor as I prevented her from hitting the floor. I caught her carbine in midair.

I swung Denise over my shoulder and ran fast as I could to the nearest and most-deserted hallway. I sat Denise against a wall.

Denise groaned with pain. "What happened?"

I pulled off my helmet. "Never mind that—we need to get you to a hospital area—now." I slid my helmet back onto my head. Denise began to cry in pain, the fullness of it coming over her. I turned away from her—I couldn't bear to look at the bloody and burnt wound.

"Call Steve," I said into my helmet. I stepped back and forth, barely able to avert my eyes to the ghastly cut on Denise's forearm. She was breathing hard, tears dripping from her nose.

Finally, "What, Josiah? I'm fighting right—"

"Now's not the time, Steve. We need to get Denise to the hospital area, NOW!"

"Oh no…" Steve panicked. "I'm coming over there. Where are you?"

"Hall A7. Get here, ASAP."

Steve hung up without saying another word. I pulled my helmet off again and bent down before Denise.

"Don't move it, Denise. There might be broken bones in there," I said, my hands shaking, fumbling with my helmet.

Steve ran from the fighting—I saw his figure bolting as fast as he could. He tore off his helmet. "How bad is it?"

"Can't you tell? Take her to the hospital as soon as you can! Now!" I was at the highest volume my vocal cords could sustain.

Steve nodded and picked up Denise, who was cradling her arm and crying in pain. I felt a surge of anger, a sudden blast, something that made me want to destroy the RED Agency. I jammed my helmet back on, reactivated my shield, and with a shout that filled my helmet, I charged through the All-Force agents and with my weapon and Denise's began to fire rapidly, not caring which direction the bolts went.

They hurt Denise…nearly killed her….

I fired, every shot my revenge for Denise's pain. Now, only a small group stood in the center of the lobby, hands on their heads, weapons on the floor.

There was a great sigh of relief from everyone. Everyone except me.

I threw my carbine, pistol, helmet, and armor on the floor, hearing them clang on the ground as they spun. The rest of the agents would examine the damage and disarm the unconscious. I had a job to do as well. I needed to tell Tom about this. He needed to know anything that might hurt the RED's "clean" reputation.

This would be a major blow.

I sat in my office, shaking. My face was pallid and cold. I felt alone. No one walked into my office to comfort me. David was probably his sister's room, hoping she would get better.

Her question to me...she hadn't know what had happened. Had she lost all memory but her pain, or was her mind just temporarily shaken from the blast?

No time to worry. Trembling I dialed Tom's code into the percom in my hands.

"Any updates?" Tom said. My heart felt crushed...he sounded almost bored.

"They launched an attack on our base."

"It's to be expected," Tom said casually. "As long as everyone was smart enough to wear shields..."

I felt even worse. "Tom, they shot Denise."

"They did *what?*" Tom's voice was as loud as it could be in my ear. I was in my office, sitting behind my desk. "You can't be serious. Is she okay?"

"She...she wasn't wearing her shield." My voice wavered. "She's being healed right now...I hope she's all right...David's with her right now." I paused, staring at the floor. I couldn't believe it either. "Where are you right now?"

"I'm in a delegation meeting as we speak. I'll make sure that they all know about this." I heard something slam.

The percom was silent. I thought that it had gone dead. "Tom?"

"I can't believe they would be this stupid. I'll call you back at the end of the meeting."

"I'll talk to you then."

The line was cut.

My chin kept shaking. But it wasn't time to sob about Denise…but no, I had to feel for her…she could have died….

The bed looked welcoming. Legs weak, I fell on the mattress. *Denise could have died. Who would have been in charge of the BLUE Agency then? Would she have been back at school in the real world, unaware of what had happened here?*

It was an hour later. I wasn't allowed to see Denise, and I hadn't received any updates on her. Tom called about the meeting—it was grim news.

"Oulaire said that it was probably a provoked attack—something that was my fault at the negotiations. Even Trenton looked surprised that he took that side on the issue, but he was able to smooth it over by agreeing."

I shook my head. "I thought Oulaire would handle this better. It looks like we're going to have to find some other way. Perhaps you could negotiate with him instead of Trenton?"

"That's what I've tried to do, but with little luck. Oulaire keeps changing the subject back so we end up negotiating with each other. Either that, or we start to argue and Oulaire stops us by changing the subject."

"That's a pity. I don't want to see the BLUE Agency end up losing this war because a stubborn general wants us to make these stupid negotiations with a group of people who don't want to negotiate. It's quite senseless." I shook my head.

"Right, I'll try to avoid his subject change in the future. Over and out, 12," Tom said. The line clicked, and the transmission ended very quickly.

I sighed and sat down. I had been pacing back and forth

as I often had when I talked with Tom in these times of the negotiations.

I would really hate to see the BLUE Agency collapse in this time of trouble. We can't afford it. We need to be here when the world sees the RED Agency in all its terror. We need to protect it. It's our world, and we need to save it before we fall into the hands of the RED Agency ourselves.

I received another call. It was from the hospital. David. My hands trembled once again as I answered.

"David! What's the latest on Denise? Is she all right? And is the wound bad, or is she going to be okay?"

"She's been doing all right…thank goodness," David said. He sounded like he had been emotional over her all afternoon. "She…she hasn't talked much since I was here. She was glad that I came, though. I'm glad too."

I felt a pang of emotion—if I hadn't been here, she wouldn't have had a brother to stand beside her hospital bed. At least, she wouldn't know it was her brother.

"Can I see her?"

"Yeah, I guess so. She's in room two ninety one in the Emergency Ward of the hospital. Come and see her if you like. Don't worry—she's bandaged up really well."

"Good—I don't want to take another look at her arm like that."

I could hear David sigh over the line. "I hope to see you in a little bit, Jones." He hung up without another word.

The hospital area was large and confusing. Signs dangled from the ceiling, directing me to places where I didn't want to go, and then it confused me by not telling me which direction the Emergency Ward was.

"Excuse me," I said to a nurse, "where is the Emergency Ward? I need to see Denise."

"Agent D is down that hall, to the left,' said the nurse pointing. "She'll be your fifth door on the right. Anything else I can do to help?"

"No, nothing in particular. Thanks, though." I walked down the hall, looking for the left turn. I kept walking. The sterile light made the skin on my arms look pale. The turn came up. I looked down the long hall. Five doors weren't too far. I strode forward slowly, trying to find the right door to enter through. There it was: fifth door on the right.

I opened it, and there was Denise, asleep, on the bed, David standing beside her. She had bandages almost across her entire arm, blood soaking through a little bit to make a small blotch of red. I squirmed at the sight of it. She looked pale.

An eye opened. She looked at me. "Josiah Jones, what are you doing here?" she said.

What if my fears were coming true? Had she forgotten about the imaginary world?

"I'm just visiting, Agent D. No major injuries?"

"None of which to speak. Just got these dang bandages on. They're using this new machine Steve's built to reconnect my bones and ligaments and help rebuild my arm."

I sighed. *So she hasn't forgotten.*

"She's been getting plenty of rest, Josiah…no need to worry," David said.

"Well…Tom's just gotten back from a meeting," I said.

"How did it go?" Denise was groggy.

"Terribly. He said that Oulaire claimed that the RED's attack must have been provoked." I gave her the details of our conversation earlier.

"That's not good," Denise said plainly.

"How did he think that? Sometimes I want to take that man and…" David punched his hand and cracked his knuckles.

I laughed, but not genuinely. We were silent.

"Are…are you in any pain?" I said. I tried to be cautious and sensitive as to not hurt Denise's feelings.

"No," she said. "It doesn't hurt with all the ointments they put all over it. Steve is a medicinal wonder. So are all the other doctors; I can see why you were in and out of the hospital so quickly last time, Josiah."

David rubbed his forehead. He looked extremely tired.

I remembered "last time" very well. I myself had been hurt in the arm when my shield overloaded, then injured again in the head when I was pistol-whipped.

"It hurt a bit more than yours, I think. Do you know if the medicine is any better now than it was before?" I asked her.

"Oh yes, substantially," she said. "We've done a lot of improvement for security and keeping our agents safe. I had to sign more paperwork to make sure extra funding went to the health sector, which was a *really* boring affair. We don't want people to be down for the count for too long when times are as unstable as they are." Denise heaved a sigh.

"Of course, we had the technology and medicine to heal you faster," David said, "but at the time we didn't have enough money to dispense on that. We've allocated some of our funds to that cause, and for that my sister is safe." David smiled.

Denise was now smiling for the first time I'd seen in several weeks. "So, how's your day been going since the battle?"

"Nervous," I said. "I was worried sick about you, then

the call from Tom about how the negotiations were going, then coming here and thinking you had lost all memory of the BLUE Agency..."

"Lost all my memory? How can one lose their memory from getting shot in the arm? For Pete's sake...there's no reason you should be complaining about how worried you were. Please, do me a favor and don't be such a baby."

I laughed again. Denise was alive and well.

CHAPTER 17: DEFENSE

Several days passed. The defense of the agency was going up, but it was going slowly...the inventors were tired between designing the B5 to making improvements to shields, weapons, and armor, and the computer programmers were working overtime to improve the Internet and firewall to keep all the agents safe from being hacked into. Everything and everyone was in hustle mode.

I spent most of my time working on the shields with Bob. He and I liked to build things like this with relatively uncomplicated parts and an easy-to-use program interface. The shields surrounded the base, planted in the field. They looked like small lamps without a light bulb. We were directed to place them in an exact circle around the base's perimeter. It was a long but easy process. We would put the ten main parts of the generator together and use the computer interface to do the rest of the programming for what the shields were going to do.

And so it went for about twenty shields. All the while, Bob and I talked.

"What do you think these shields are going to do? Make people bounce off the agency headquarters?" I said with a laugh.

"Yeah, well, they're said to provide a good electric shock to anyone who doesn't have the password to open them. They said that on the newest armor release they're going to have a keypad on the wrist to type in the deactivation password."

"What would happen if a RED agent were to walk in while the shield was deactivated?" I said.

"It's not the shield that gets deactivated per se...it's the shield being turned off to that certain device or person. It detects whether it's coming from a car or a person, and lets that car or person through the shield without being harmed. Plus it's almost invisible, so there's no way they'll see what's coming."

"Denise also said that Steve's invented a machine for making bones reconnect."

"Yeah, he did that a few months ago. I think it aligns the bone like a cast, and you consume a lot of calcium to rebuild the bone and protein for the muscle."

I put the last part onto a shield generator I was working on.

"So, what can you tell me about why you work at the BLUE Agency?" I asked.

"Well..." Bob hesitated. "It's a really long story, but I guess we have time, don't we?"

"I have all the time in the world. Shoot!" I had cut my finger on the edge of one of the spikes to put into the ground.

"Well…my family…government runs in their blood. My dad was related to a former governor of New York…I believe that was his uncle. And my mom used to work in the police force, just to name my parents. I have more cousins that work in agencies like this. Some of them can't even tell me who they work for."

"Cool. I wish I had that kind of family."

"Yeah, I guess. And my brother is a senator for Indiana."

"How does your family get so involved with the government?"

"Well, they've just been doing it for so long that it's inevitable that at any one time someone in my family is bound to be in the government."

"Wow. How many years have you been in the BLUE again?" I asked. I finished the programming and pressed the accept button on the machine.

"It's kind of hard to remember because most of my life I have been here. It must have been when I was four or five that I started training, but I can't quite recall. Hmm…" Bob thought, and I continued to work tirelessly. It was a tedious job. My fingers felt numb from piecing the parts together, and I was getting a headache from doing the same thing over and over and over again. It felt like listening to the same annoying song multiple times for hours on end. Without Bob's conversation, I felt like I was being eaten alive by boredom. I waited for him to say something.

"I sort of remember…it was like I was coming here for kindergarten, except it was a highly specialized kindergarten. I would be trained in math, science, reading, writing…and then I was taught military things like infiltration and how to use the technology and all that other stuff we did. It was sort of like your basic training only a bit less complicated because I was only five. Do you get it?"

"Yeah, I see. So...you've been here for quite a while then?"

"Yes. Exited basic training at age nine. At least I think I exited at age 9...I'd have to check the records."

"How often do you see your parents?" I asked.

"All the time. They live only a few blocks away and they visit me often. If you come into my office on most weekdays, they'll be there for about an hour. It's nice having them live so close."

"Do you see your brother, the one who's a representative?"

"Not too often," Bob said. He picked up the first and second pieces of a generator and stuck them together. "I see him every once in a while, say, every month or two. But he's often busy. It's not like I resent him for it, he's a cool guy. I like hanging out with him and I knew him pretty well before he moved away."

"That's good," I said. "Why would you say your parents put you in the BLUE instead of some other thing, like, regular school?"

"I'd have to say because I was able to do a lot of really good stuff like math and talking when I was very young. I learned to read when I was two and started reading chapter books when I was four. I think they thought that I needed military training because I was also very loyal to my country."

"How could they tell if you were loyal at age five?"

"Who knows? They got it down pretty well. I love it here, and I would die for the BLUE Agency."

"I agree," I said with confidence in my voice. "You do

some risky things sometimes, even if David or Denise tells you not to. Although some of those things may not be smart..." My voice smacked of sarcasm, and Bob could tell.

"Quit jabbering about how I always get in trouble, will you?" Bob said. He smiled. "Besides, I'm not always the one getting in trouble. There are other people who get caught at doing bad stuff more often than I do."

"Name five."

"I don't want to go into names right now. But some people have been removed from the BLUE Agency for doing a number of very stupid things that I would never do, like infiltrating other bases in their own agency to steal money. That's not even cool. Can you see me doing that?"

I sarcastically looked thoughtful as I pieced two parts together to form a nearly-completed shield generator.

"Oh, come on."

"I'm just kidding!"

Someone leaped from a hatch in the field. I turned on a dime—KC.

"What is it, KC? Can't you see we're working?"

She breathed rapidly and her face was red. "Plan to attack the BLUE base. Soon. Hurry to Denise's office, both of you. I can take this job."

"Are you sure you can handle it?" I asked.

KC took a quick breather "Yes, I'm fine. I read the manual, so I think I'm primed and set. I'm afraid you won't have a happy time in Denise's office."

I slid down the same hatch that KC had come up from, which was less than a stone's throw from Denise's office. Running across the hall, we heard the footsteps of Denise as she paced across the floor.

The door slid open, and I sat down at the white seat that she had set up across from a single one that she was walking toward.

"You can sit down, Bob," she said slowly. Her arm was still bandaged, but not as thickly as it had been a few days ago. The gauze was not blood-spotted as it had been before.

"Give us the details," I said. Denise looked worn and tired.

"One of our Internet programmers who was working on the firewall intercepted a misrouted e-mail detailing the events in this attack."

"And what did it describe?" I asked. The surge of knowledge that what she was saying now was going to happen in mere days was disconcerting at best.

I miss having time for myself, time to look up at the sky. I wish that I could be out of this place, this stupid imaginary world. But I've made a pact—I can't leave without being ridiculed for years. I can face this.

I looked at Denise.

"The RED Agency has certain entrances they're going to focus on with a lot of troops. And…it looks like they're assuming that Oulaire will be on their side." Denise was somber.

I quivered slightly but noticeably. I hoped she wouldn't think I was nervous, so I said with artificial strength, "So that's why Trenton has been pulling him aside at the end of meetings—he's been trying to give himself an extra boost by becoming buddies with Oulaire. I still think there's money involved." I filled my voice with disgust.

"What?" Denise said. "He's still been talking to Oulaire, alone?"

"Far as I know, he has been," I said. "This means we have

to feed this to Tom and make sure Oulaire finds out about the RED's plot."

"No." Denise pounded her fist on her chair's arm.

"What?" I said. "But how are we going to win their favor if…"

"Don't you see? They'd know that we know about their plans if we stated it in front of the likes of Trenton." Denise was almost at the yelling point.

I thought for a moment. "You're right in that," I said, "but what if he only told Oulaire?"

Denise was suddenly quiet. "We can't trust anyone right now, Josiah. Not Oulaire. Not Trenton. There are people who very badly want to see the BLUE Agency go up in smoke. I'm not one of them."

"And we can't even trust Tom?" I said. I turned my head to face Bob, whose brow was furrowed and eyes intently staring at his feet.

Denise sighed heavily. "Yes, I think we can trust Tom. He's been with us for…a while. And he has Bryan and Gary to back him up—tell Tom to keep it within the BLUE agents there, no one else."

I nodded. *We can't trust anyone but the BLUE Agency. How can this be good?*

"And you, Bob, you are in charge of distributing the information of where you are to go when the attack is launched to every person in Regiment Washington and other Midwest and Eastern Sea Board All-Force regiments. I will tell them to report to you." Denise sighed once again. If I had ever seen her unhappy, this beat every other time.

Bob rolled his eyes…he had the boring job.

"So, Josiah," Denise said, "you will contact Tom and tell

him about this, and Bob, you will distribute the pages to everyone in your regiment and the other regiments specified."

"What do I look like, a secretary?" Bob said.

"We don't have secretaries for every agent," Denise said patiently. And inconveniently mine was on vacation while she was supposed to be stamping applications with my signature." Denise folded her hands. "Well, you are dismissed."

Bob stood up and started to walk away.

"Oh! Sorry, I forgot. Bob?" Denise said.

Bob turned around.

"You'll need this." Denise picked up a box under her desk. It was full of file folders, which were full of pieces of paper nicely and evenly printed.

Bob walked out with the box, considerably slowed by its weight. I started to follow.

"Josiah, I'd like to have a word with you," Denise said as I stepped in front of the door.

"Yes?" I said, walking back.

"You know what I said about not being able to trust anyone outside of the BLUE Agency?"

"Yeah," I said. "Why is that? Can't we trust anybody?"

"I meant what I said. In essentially every crime syndicate there is at least one RED agent. They've made sure of that. And if you happen to let something slip to an undercover syndicate member…"

"Don't worry. I'll keep discreet about the BLUE Agency."

"I hope so, Jones, I hope so."

CHAPTER 18: TIMES MORE DESPERATE

I called Tom on my percom, thinking, *we can't trust any-one outside the BLUE. Can't trust anyone....*

"Yo, Jo," said Tom.

"No time." My voice wavered. "Listen…the RED is planning to launch a full-scale wipeout attack on the BLUE again."

"You can't be serious," Tom said. "Are you making all this up so we can get the GREEN on our side? It would seem pretty bizarre that—"

I broke him off. "I'm not a liar. You know that. They're planning a full-scale assault. The massacre was just a sign of what was to come. I was right in thinking that we needed to prepare defensively."

"What am I supposed to do with this information?"

"This means that you need to speed up. Expedite. Hurry.

Go as fast as you can. Whatever phrase you prefer. Use any persuasion methods possible to get Oulaire on our side. This is our most desperate time, and we need you to come through for us, Tom." My voice came out more frantic and less composed than I had imagined.

A sigh. "Okay, I'll do what I can, Josiah. I won't let you down."

"And Tom," I said.

"What?"

"Don't tell anyone but a legitimate BLUE agent about this. Otherwise, we're dead."

"Gotcha. Over and out."

He hung up, and I sat with a plunk onto my bed, throwing the percom at my pillow. What were we going to do? And why was I staying? *I know this doesn't all come down to me,* I thought, *but it sure feels like it. What can I do for my agency?*

Everything was even more flurried in the following days. Now that we knew that an attack was coming, it was the subject of every conversation and it was constantly on everyone's mind. "What's going to happen during the attack? What group are you in? Which entrance have you been assigned to guard?"

All these questions bombarded me endlessly and began to give me a headache, walking through the day, going to lunch and sitting far away from the questioners, and working out at the gym. However far away I was from these people, they seemed to find me and ask me (some of them multiple times). Like a team endlessly dumping Gatorade on an already-drenched coach.

Bob gave me our assignment: Door A4, one of the most

guarded doors in the entire building. And for good reason, too. It was vulnerable to almost any kind of attack because the door was made of pure Plexiglas, and it was a backdoor to the lobby, where most attackers usually wanted to begin their marauding.

I was working overtime on that stupid shield generator, trying to get all the individual components up, or at least as many as possible to make sure that they were effective. This wasn't really a necessity since other people were already working on it, but it was a distraction to get me away from all the annoying question bombardiers.

Sometimes I would hide myself in my bedroom and watch the clouds move across my ceiling, remembering times as a child when my friends and I would lie out sprawled on a grassy hilltop and imagine what it would be like to soar between the clouds until we would close our eyes and nap on the soft grass….

But then I would be harshly awoken by a message on my percom or someone walking into my room and the illusion would fade.

Even worse than the bombardiers were the rumor spreaders. The number-one rumor was that the tech manager who had discovered the e-mail had written it himself and was actually a RED agent trying to fool us, but it was only a rumor and was never found out to be true.

The shield generator now had five people working on it, including KC, Bob and I, who stayed together as a group. We built the generators three at a time, one for each person, and talked.

We tried to keep our conversation away from the deadly situation for which we were preparing, but it inevitably came back to how much we wanted the battle to stop sucking up all our free time and demanding every bit of energy from us so that when we went to bed at ten or eleven o'clock, we had been ready since 6 o'clock.

Denise wasn't doing much better. She had a truckload of tasks she was assigned to do from the leaders of the regiments, which was partially her fault. Each regiment turned in their progress reports of how they were building their defenses to the division, and the division turned in the collective project report to Denise, who then had to spend days on end simply reading some reports on progress people were making through the work they did, which was often excruciatingly monotonous.

The days passed, and they passed slowly. I hated it. And every day, I would call Tom to check on the progress with the negotiations.

"Any updates, Tom?" I said, picking up the percom.

"Great news!" Tom said.

"What?" Had Oulaire finally consented to come with the BLUE Agency and defend us? What was going to happen now? Would we win the negotiation and cause the RED to cancel their attack?

"We've made Oulaire say that he was going to defend one and attack the other," Tom said excitedly.

The smile disappeared from my face. "Tom, isn't that just a sign that he's going to choose the RED?" I said. There was audible disappointment in my voice.

"But it means we still have a shot, doesn't it?"

"Yeah, I guess," I said. I felt better—at least Oulaire had openly admitted that we had a shot. "So, uh...did you say anything about the RED attack?"

"Yeah," Tom said. "I told Gary, Bryan, Oulaire—"

"Whoa, whoa, whoa…hold the phone! You told Oulaire about the attack?"

"Don't worry," Tom said, relaxed. "I was alone with him at the time."

"You're sure there was no one else in the room?"

"Well, the waiter…"

"Ha, ha, ha. Funny. Still…he could have leaked that information to the RED agent. They're getting to be too close of friends."

Tom sighed. "I doubt he'll tell. But in the meantime… how is it going at the base? Are you making preparations?"

"We have the shield generator up and running. We just have to get the new armor out so we can put it up and have it going in plenty of time for the attack."

"That's good. How's the armor coming along, then?" he asked. I could tell he was pretty happy, even though they were barely even anywhere as far as the negotiations went.

"The armor is almost finished. They're just telling the computers how to program them to use the passwords."

"Good. I like the way they think. Do they have the cloth that absorbs the energy yet?"

"No. They just don't have time to come up with that material. We'll just have to do with the stronger fiber and the shields. Besides…the shields shouldn't blow anyway. It blocks every shot that we've tried on it."

"Yeah, you're right," Tom said. "I'm going to have to go. It's dinner and negotiation time. I hope to be able to bring you good news soon about how we've won over the GREEN Agency!"

And then, over the next few days, everyone had been over-clocking. And that meant a lot more got done a lot more quickly. We had almost everything completed at around week 2 of the 2 months that we had to prepare for the attack.

One day, out of nowhere, I got a call on my percom from Agent D. I picked it up.

"What do you need?"

"I'm desperate," she spat.

"What is it? Is there trouble?" I stood and impulsively reached for a carbonyssium carbine I kept by my bedside.

"No, it's just that I need to get away from these progress reports!" she yelled. "It's like teaching a manatee how to drive: repetitive, fruitless, and dangerous to your health."

"What do you want me to do about it?"

"I need someone to hang out with—take a break from all this stuff that's going on. I need some relaxation."

Well, I do *need some R and R.*

"Sure," I said. "I'll be there in a few. Want anyone else to come?"

"Not this time. I want to talk to you about some stuff."

"Um…okay; thanks for being specific."

Denise hung up unexpectedly, and without further ado, I walked out of the room.

It was only fifteen minutes later, and Denise and I were laughing in the Seclab.

She had been so bored with her progress reports and had felt so mindless that she had accidentally shredded twelve of them in her paper shredder along with some junk papers she had on her desk.

"Good job," I said, taking a green soda out of the cold

refrigerator. I popped open the tab and took a long draw.

"I know…I can be pretty stupid sometimes." She laughed. "To my own stupidity!" I met the toast with my can and took another swig.

"So, what was it that you really wanted to talk about?" I asked.

"Um, well…" Denise swirled her soda around nervously. "I'm almost afraid to talk about it."

"What is the general subject?"

"My brother."

Denise referring to David as "my brother" made me feel uncomfortable. "He has a name, you know."

"I don't like talking about it. It still makes me feel jittery to think that for so long he was my brother, and for years I was his enemy. But now it's kind of weird. We talk all the time and we can hug without it being weird and he's my confidant all of a sudden."

"Continue."

"I want to meet him in real life, Josiah. Where he lives. I think it would be really cool to do that sometime, but I don't know how we're going to pull that off." Denise leaned on the couch.

"I know he lives in Ohio in reality. What part?"

"Up north, near Cleveland, he said," she said.

"My parents have some friends there that we're going to be visiting over summer break this year. We could take you and sneak off to meet David." I refused to call him "Denise's brother." I knew him as David, and I had even imagined him as such. I wasn't going to change just because Denise was too uncomfortable with the name and association with her own kinship.

"Are you serious?" I sensed suspicion and quickly put up my guard.

"Yeah, I think we could ask him about his phone number. Do you have a cell phone we could use? My parents haven't given me one yet."

"I have one, but I wish I could bring my percom into the real world." Denise was distracted. "It would be way better than my normal cell phone."

"How so? Don't cell phones have better capabilities?"

"No, not nearly as many," Denise said. "Didn't you know that? It's in the little white book."

I felt stupid for not knowing once again. "Of course, everything is in the little white book. The one that I keep forgetting to read!"

Denise just laughed and took another drink of her soda. "You have a copy somewhere in your room."

"Can you just tell me what features it has?"

"It pretty much has every feature you would find on a smart phone, and then some military abilities as well. If you look on the back, there's a touch-screen module that you can use if you need to," Denise said with a grin. "Or you can just use the good old QWERTY keyboard and numbers on the other side. Either way is fine, but the touch screen is where it really gets cool."

I didn't know that percoms had a touch screen.

"And they are able to act as a bomb when all else fails, though they're not very powerful. They'd only knock someone out for an hour at the most."

"That's still a powerful phone," I said. "Remarkable. So, all the features of a cell phone times ten?"

"Pretty much."

Denise was receiving a call on her percom. She picked it up. "Hello?"

"We've received an urgent message. The RED know that we know that they're coming."

Suddenly it hit me as I heard the booming and angry voice on the other end of Denise's call. I froze.

"How could they have known that it was intercepted?" Denise's voice was filled with a sudden fear that I'd never heard her have.

"Apparently they were expecting a response and never got it, and found that they had misrouted the e-mail in our direction."

I still sat, stunned. They didn't even know how it had happened.

I did.

"I forwarded an e-mail to you—it was from Frederick. He decided to scare us himself with his own personal e-mail. I hope you can get it as soon as possible. It has important information that we can't let past us."

"Got it. Over and out, sir."

She hung up and wrapped her head in her arms.

"Denise," I said slowly.

"What?" Denise didn't move.

"They…they weren't expecting a response. That's not how they found out." I gulped hard.

"What? How else could they have known?"

"Tom…Tom told Oulaire."

CHAPTER 19: MEASURES MOST DRASTIC

"I can't believe it," she said.

"I told him he shouldn't have!" I said.

"I know...I trust that you did," Anger seeped into her voice. "But...I can't believe that Tom would do something like this. What exactly did you say to him to keep him from telling anyone else?"

"I told him not to tell anyone but a legit BLUE agent."

"You didn't mention that Oulaire was out of bounds?"

I was silent for a moment. "No," I said in a small voice. "Denise, what are we going to do?" I started to tremble.

"Quit panicking! I'm tired of you constantly worrying about every little thing! Can't you stay calm every once in a while? Yes, this is an unmitigated disaster, but we have to keep cool."

"Sorry."

"Ah...I'm not keepin' my cool!" Denise's whole body trembled and twitched.

Denise hurried up the secret stairway into her main office. She was panting. Hastily she logged on her computer, failing several times to correctly type her password because of her urgency.

All the while I was thinking to myself...*why did Tom do that? He unwittingly sold us to the RED Agency. Gave away our ace in the hole. But I guess "unwittingly" is the key word there.* I sighed deeply.

Frederick's e-mail showed the truth. I glanced at the title: "*You were fooled.*"

"I bet it's just a scare tactic, a ploy to make us think that they didn't mean to send the e-mail at all. Well, it is consistent with their character..."

"Please, can your mouth remain shut for a *second*? It's like your jaw is a squeaky hinge that won't shut." I ignored this, considering the situation.

She clicked on the message.

"*You have been fooled, BLUE Agency!*" the first line read.

"It's unpredictable already," I said.

"Shut up!" she snapped.

"*The e-mail you received has now been canceled. We are no longer running the operation outlined in said e-mail. We are going to attack when you least expect it, strike when you know it not. You will die in agony because you will ignore this e-mail and not care if we attack. The GREEN Agency is on our side. We've made special arrangements to take care of that. There is nothing you can do to stop us. Goodbye.*

Signed,

Frederick."

My face turned pallid. Denise's lips were shut tight. I saw anger in her face. "They must be telling the truth," I said shakily.

"Don't worry—it's probably just a stupid scare tactic to take us in. Tom can get the GREEN on our side." I sensed false confidence.

"I wouldn't be so confident. We'd better check this out as soon as possible," I retorted.

"Don't be such a worrier. You call Tom and we can have this all sorted out in no time. Okay? Okay. Now, if you'll pardon me, I have some work to do here."

Walking out of the room, I dialed Tom's code with shaking fingers. What if the e-mail wasn't just to be a threat? What if they had really turned the mind of Jean Claude de Oulaire? What if they were to assassinate Tom?

To my relief, the latest of these fears was not true. Tom picked up his percom and answered plainly, "Hey, Josiah." He sounded unusually dim and despondent.

"What's wrong?" I said.

"Oh, nothing, it's just that these negotiations are getting stressful. Oulaire can't make up his mind. It makes me want to punch him in the face or something. Then I think, 'You know, he's far too big for me to take on,' and then I just get depressed and sound like I'm Eeyore."

"That's a long explanation," I blurted, unable to think of a witty retort. "But we have critical news. The RED Agency has *somehow* heard about how the e-mail was misrouted and they've canceled their plans of attack. They are going to attack whenever they want to."

"Are you ready over there?" Tom sounded genuinely worried now. However, he seemed oblivious to my implication that he had sold us to the RED.

"We're not really prepared for an attack at any moment, and if we get the troops ready right now, they'll be on edge for the entire time. I mean…they'll be angry if the attack doesn't happen right away. Do you get what I'm saying?" I said, raising my voice.

"Yeah, I hear you. They'll have anger issues," he said. He sounded like he himself was angry, but I didn't want to go too deep into that.

"How are we going to convince the GREEN Agency to our side, though?" I said. "The e-mail we got said that the RED Agency has convinced him to their side. And Oulaire has been having those…secret meetings with Trenton. I think that they're telling the truth. They're really on the side of the RED."

"What?" Tom said. "That's not true."

"But of course you would know that he was for the side of the RED! Oh, yeah, you're the expert! *Because you sold us to them!*" The dam of anger that had been building since I had left Denise's office burst. "And furthermore, why didn't you stop their meetings? You're perfectly able!"

"Whoa! Hold on, Josiah! I…I didn't think you meant that I couldn't tell Oulaire. I…I thought it would help our chances." His voice was calm, not angry, not fearful, not as I had hoped. The fires in my mind began to cool.

"I…well, I'm sorry Tom. I shouldn't have done that. But please, follow instructions *to the letter* next time. Well, technically they were Denise's instructions, but for all intents and purposes—"

"Good idea. I'll definitely remember that for the future." He sounded genuine, earnest.

"Good."

"All right…well, see you later, partner."

"What did you call me partner for?"

"Heh. Over and out, Jo."

The line clicked and the transmission ended. I shook my head. Where did they dig up that guy?

I was back in my own room, looking up at the sky. I stared at the cloudless simulation, contemplating the day's events. The sun was shining down, and it actually felt hot on my face. I decided to turn down the temperature amounts on my computer. It didn't need to be this realistic.

"Computer," I said.

"Yes, Mr. Jones?" the computer answered. I liked having something answer me as "Mr. Jones," even if it was a digital voice

"Can you turn down the temperature realism for the Stars application? It doesn't need to be this realistic. Not too far down, though…I don't want to freeze to death, either."

"All right, Mr. Jones."

The temperature lowered to a comfortable 70 degrees Fahrenheit.

I sat there in my chair and smiled. I liked having the Stars application. I would have to thank Steve in person for inventing such a wonderful program.

I was waiting for the call from Denise to say that everyone in the agency had been notified of the e-mail and that everyone was getting ready for war. There would be shifts taken for guarding each entrance according to the former plan—it was all that we had to go off of. It may have not been exactly accurate, but it was good enough to prepare for the attack. I just crossed my fingers and hoped that the entrances we guarded the least wouldn't be the ones they attacked the most.

Finally, my percom beeped signaling Denise's awaited call. "Hello, Denise…do you have everyone notified?" I was already wearing the new and improved armor for being ready at a moments notice.

"Yes. You know the instructions, right?" she said with a nervous tone.

"When you go to sleep, have all your stuff waiting by the bed. Keep your armor and shields on you at all times. Take your three-hour shift guarding your assigned door every day. Thank you for cooperating and helping the BLUE Agency keep its agents and the world safe."

Denise laughed at my recitation. "Good job," she said. "I wish every agent was as prepared as you are."

I smiled sheepishly. "Well…hearing it so many times I wanted to stuff my head into a trash can helped a bit…"

Denise laughed again. "Thanks for cheering up my day. But seriously, we need to be ready at a moment's notice. Are you prepared to do that?"

"I am," I said, picking up the serious tone for my voice. "I hate that they had to find out about this stupid misrouted e-mail. It's a good thing we knew about it, though. We needed to over clock or else we would have never been ready for this attack. How are those progress reports coming along?"

"Screw progress reports! We need to get ready for action. I was the one who ordered for the progress reports anyway, so I don't really have any trouble abolishing them." I could almost see her face as she rolled her eyes, an expression I knew all too well.

"Heh. You're funny. By the way…Tom said he's going to

try to fix the situation...you know, negotiations and all..." It came out a bit shakily like I was nervous. I think Denise heard that, but didn't want to mention it.

"Well, we'll all have to do the best we can to keep this agency intact."

For a few moments there was an uncomfortable silence. "I think that everyone at the negotiations is probably unhappy that I left," I said.

"Why?"

"Well...I was sort of the one that they 'chose' to be the delegate. Or something like that. I don't know why they expected me to have nothing else to do. And the fact that they invited me so late...I don't know."

"I didn't hear about this. You'll have to tell me more sometime. I have to do something else, I'm sure."

Denise's evasiveness disturbed me. "Okay. Well...see you later."

I hung up, not knowing what else to say.

I waited for Tom's call. Out of boredom, I was sitting at my computer and clicking the check mail button in my e-mail. It was almost always empty.

Until there popped up an e-mail. It was addressed from Frederick...no, it couldn't be. Frederick of the RED Agency. The title read "Be Warned."

Eyes squinted, I clicked on the message.

"*Dear Mr. Jones,*

"*I think you are going to regret your decision to leave Paris. That way your little friend Tom may live to see tomorrow. He might have, if you would have risked your own life. But that doesn't matter anymore. He'll be dead by morning. Sayonara, sir.*

Signed,

Frederick."

I clicked away from the e-mail, angered by the sickness of the man's mind. I would have to wait for the call to find out if he was telling the truth. It was due to be here any second now.

Ten minutes.

Fifteen.

Twenty five.

A whole half hour had passed before I reasoned with myself to just call Tom.

"What are you calling me for, Josiah? I was about to call you to tell you about what Oulaire said."

I breathed a great sigh of relief. "Thank goodness! I just received an e-mail saying that there's a plot to kill you. You need to get out of Paris, ASAP."

"What?" Tom said. "Who was the e-mail from?"

"Frederick. And I don't think he was lying this time."

CHAPTER 20: DEATH RACE

"Why would they want a plot to kill me, of all people? No offense, but I can see why they would kill you, but I feel like a pretty insignificant piece of the puzzle here."

"Insignificant? Doesn't make sense? It makes perfect sense! You're the delegate for the BLUE Agency! With you out of the way, it wouldn't be a fight to win over the GREEN Agency. And without a good advocate on our side, they could win him over very quickly…more quickly than now, if that's at all possible. And it's probably also to instill fear in the rest of the BLUE."

"Wouldn't Oulaire be appalled that the RED had killed me to get their way?"

"No," I said. "They would just cover up the fact that it was a murder. Say that 'he was attacked by a criminal' or something. Nothing of their doing. Or maybe that you had left the country because it was too hard to negotiate. Heck, as far as we know, the GREEN is involved in it too.He"

"This isn't good. We have a negotiation at dinner…and this will have to be the last one if what you say is true. Tell Denise to have a plane arranged, right after dinner. No exceptions."

"I'll tell her straightaway. Do whatever you can to convince Oulaire. It's all coming down to you now."

"Right. Over and out."

"Don't do anything stupid! I'll send you the info as soon as I have it. Be safe, and keep your guard up. Tell Bryan and Gary to be safe too. We don't want anyone to be affected by this, even if it's just a threat. We can't afford to assume anything. And Tom?"

"Huh?"

"Give me a live video feed."

"Got it. Over and out."

Perhaps he sounded a bit annoyed this time. I didn't care.

"Over and out."

The line was cut, and my stomach was left churning—almost sick. Trenton was probably going to try something at dinner tonight. The very idea brought impulses to retch. I quickly remembered the task at hand.

I dialed for Agent D.

"Josiah? Why are you calling now?"

"I just got an e-mail…there's a death threat over Tom. He's in great danger. He's on his way to his last negotiation tonight at dinner…and I think Trenton is going to do the dirty deed himself. Get a plane arranged as soon as possible."

"Why would they make a death threat for Tom? That

seems ludicrous," Denise said.

"Would you just shut up and listen for once? This is Tom's life on the line and you're saying it's ludicrous. Just do what I said and get the plane."

"We only have one other plane available in Paris right now. You're in luck, and so is Tom."

"Good." I felt relief surge, but anger and disgust toward Trenton still welled. "We need it, and we need it now."

I stared intently my monitor, watching the video feed. Nerves tingling, heart barely pushing a pulse. Tom sat down at the table. He wasn't going to be eating this time at dinner. He had more important things to discuss.

"Good evening," he said as he seated himself. I wondered if they would go through with the plan, if seven or so RED agents would burst into the room and kill him, or if Trenton will discretely shoot him from underneath the table. These were all horrifying thoughts.

"As you all know," Tom said shakily, "I have to leave right after this meeting, so I will not be able to dine with you. This shall be our last negotiation."

"What?" Oulaire said, who actually was unaware of the fact that Tom was leaving that very evening. "How...why are you leaving? First Mr. Jones, and now you...we cannot go on with the negotiations like this!"

"That's my point," Tom said harshly. "The negotiations end, and they end tonight. I have been told to come home and I certainly will."

Tom twiddled his thumbs for a few seconds until someone said something.

"You know that the RED Agency has far more power

than the BLUE," Trenton said confidently.

"That's not always the deciding matter in times of war," said the general calmly. He looked introspective, trying to think...think of what he should do. He almost looked like he was sealing the deal in his mind.

He made a grim expression toward the BLUE side of the table. "Anything you have to say, BLUE Agency, in favor of your side?"

"We are working for the good of the people of the world, and the only problem we have encountered is the RED Agency!" Gary blurted.

"Sh!" Tom said. "Don't say that sort of outright—"

He had no time to finish. "That's a very foolishly worded sentence," Trenton said. "We are not the only problem you have encountered. What about organized crime groups? Aren't they a hazard to you?"

"And your agency runs most of the organized crime in the world! You have members from almost every major gang in every major country in the world. And you have top agents in the Mafia in every—"

"That's enough," said Oulaire. He was extremely calm. He aimed a foul expression in the direction of Tom, Bryan and Gary.

"What? Why should we stop negotiating? Isn't that what we're here for?" Tom sounded confused.

"No. You don't need to debate. There's no time for that," Oulaire said, "because I have already made up my mind."

My heart leapt.

"What?" Trenton said.

"What?" Tom, Gary, and Bryan said in unison. "After so many days of being indecisive and hating the idea of siding with one—" Tom's rant was stopped.

"Because," Oulaire chose his words carefully, "I was convinced by their side of the argument. It was your last few statements that closed it in my mind."

"So, who is it?" said Trenton impatiently.

Oulaire smiled slyly. "Please, we don't have time for this. I think you will be able to tell whom I chose by what I command my people to do." With that, he picked up a device that looked like a more austere and sophisticated version of a percom. "Send four Centurion armies to the RED Agency's base, please." He looked angrily at the BLUE side of the table as he said this.

I knew it! I thought.

Tom made his decision right then. He was getting out. He bolted up out of his seat and ran for the door, holding the small camera in his hand. Bryan and Gary followed closely behind. I saw the hotel-like carpet in a blur, and Tom's Chuck Taylors as he desperately ran for home.

Trenton stood up. "No! General, you can't let them escape!" He fired two shots just as the bulletproof door was closed. He was alone in the room with Jean Claude Oulaire.

"You let them go!" I heard Trenton shout behind the door.

"I don't care. It doesn't matter—we're sending our agents to your headquarters anyway. Be happy."

Tom exited the building through the old house they had come in after searching for the same button Broc had pushed. Gary and Bryan were almost constantly behind him. They flashed ID's as government agents at a car rental and were now speeding toward the secret airport just outside of Paris. All the time, I stared with terror at my screen.

Tom, Bryan and Gary were in the car, all their stuff hastily thrown into the back. "We have to warn the BLUE! The GREEN is now our enemy," Gary yelled.

Tom attempted to call Josiah. "Agh! It isn't working! It says 'access blocked.' "

"Oh please say it doesn't say that," Bryan said.

"Why would I lie to you?"

"That means they've blocked our communications! They can't reach us, and we can't reach them." Bryan's voice was grave. "At least we can use the camera. But we don't know if he can see us anymore…"

"Screw that, then. Let's book!" Tom put the pedal to the metal and they sped off in a rented car.

I wanted to tell them I could see, that every move they made was monitored, but I was forced to watch them drive away from the GREEN at breakneck pace.

"Do we all have armor, shields and weapons?" said Bryan.

"I have mine," Gary said.

"Wearing it," Tom replied.

"Good. We need to be ready as soon as we get to the airport to take some shots. I think we can get these guys down if we follow Josiah's instructions from last time."

"And what were those?" Tom asked.

"Aim for the areas where it's just cloth. Then we can get them down without having to worry about their armor."

"Right," Tom said assuredly. He was ready to hop out of the car at the moment they arrived at the airport. "Glad communications weren't blocked before the meeting. What would we have done then?"

The car seemed to travel slower than any car they had ever ridden in. They waited for the airport to come into view, gated by a chain-link fence.

Tom finally pulled in and drove through the open gateway into the parking lot. There was a single airplane waiting there, and the pilot and staff were outside, holding their hands to their heads in surrender to six RED agents who were lined up in front of them, guns drawn.

A surge of anger went through me. The RED and the GREEN were both against us now—what could we do?

Tom skidded the car behind the plane on the runway. Nearly wrenching the door off the car, he leapt out and began firing, missing half the time. Bryan and Gary were close to him. The RED agents attempted to shoot down the airplane and airport personnel in front of them, but before they knew it, Tom, Bryan, and Gary were defending them.

"Go! Get in the plane!" Tom shouted to the crew, who promptly obeyed. The camera remained securely locked to his belt.

There were more than originally seen, as usual. But they didn't seem to be there to kill him...they were almost all down now. Suddenly there was a blast, an explosion from inside the hangar. There were more inside, and their prospects for survival were not looking good.

CHAPTER 21: REVELATION

Tom was torn. Jump on the plane to safety, or save the people in the hangar?

In another burst of passion, he ran up the stairs and closed the door to the plane to keep the staff safe. Running and shooting at the same time, he glided across the runway and toward the hangar.

"Tom! What are you doing?" Bryan shouted.

"There are people inside! I have to get the RED agents in the hangar! You guys defend the plane!"

Tom rushed inside the hanger, the door swinging shut behind him. The giant garage-door was closed, leaving no real escape route for the agents inside.

To Tom's horror, there were bombs set with forty seconds left on the walls. They were going to take the place down.

A red alert light was flashing overhead. Tom had no time

to think. There were the RED agents—guns raised at the airport agents.

Tom sneaked around behind a helicopter, gun over the tail, hidden. First RED agent, down with the squeeze of a trigger. Second agent didn't know what hit him. In five seconds, all six RED agents were on the ground.

"Everybody out!" Tom shouted. The airport agents ran as fast as they could toward the exit, hurrying one by one through the door.

Tom knew what he had to do.

Fifteen seconds left.

Tom picked up all three of the RED agents in one surge of adrenaline, slinging their unconscious bodies over his back. He ran with all his might to the door.

Ten seconds.

Feet pounding on the metal floor....

Five seconds.

Trying to wrench open the door...getting out....

Zero seconds.

The entire hangar exploded in fury. I almost could feel the intense heat singe his neck as he bolted from the collapsing building. He flipped off his feet, sprawling forward with the people on his back falling forward.

Breathing heavily, Tom released the burden of the RED soldiers from his back, far away from the explosion. His shield was flickering. It wasn't meant to withstand this.

"The hangar staff should be able to take their weapons," Tom said. "We've gotta go."

The plane door opened, and Bryan and Gary boarded. Tom followed, but stood in the doorway long enough to shout to the remaining agents, "Make sure these RED agents are taken for questioning."

One of the pilots saluted to Tom. And you know, I swear there was a tear in that man's eye.

"Tom," Gary said as Tom closed the door.

"Huh?"

"That was the bravest act you could have done in that situation. Now those agents owe you their lives…both BLUE and RED."

Tom smiled wide. "Thanks, man. Thanks."

The plane departed Paris, and though Tom was happy that he had done something to save the BLUE, he knew that someone was going to be there. Someone was going to try to kill him again.

I was waiting, waiting all morning, afternoon and into the night for a call—some sign that they landed all right. I needed something to hang on to assure me that we had the GREEN Agency on our side. If we didn't, they needed to run like heck and get back here in time to save their skins. If we did, then we would have already won and the RED Agency might as well give up.

But no call came. By ten o'clock, I was fast asleep.

Suddenly, the percom beeped. There was someone trying to contact me. Who could it be? Was it Tom? Gary? Bryan? Any of those options would have put me at ease, but no. It was just a call from Denise. Maybe they called her, I thought. Maybe she was so excited that she had to tell me….

"Hello? What do you need, Agent D?"

"I have received contact from the plane. They're landing in an hour, and I want you, David, and Bob to be there to pick them up."

"You got a call? How come I didn't get one? Did they say the outcome of the final negotiation?"

There was silence over the line. "They're sending a hundred men to the RED Agency headquarters. I received a message from a spy we have there that the RED are due to attack in three days."

I hung my head in despair. "So, that's the end of the BLUE Agency then. We have lost. We'll have to go back to the ordinary world. Or whatever happens to us when we die here…"

"I don't know what will happen, Josiah, but we should be optimistic. We need to push through whatever obstacles may be in our way. Those agents are probably just to defend the RED base from attack, not to attack us. All hope is not lost."

"I don't share your optimism," I said. I shook my head. "We're done for. There's nobody who can beat the GREEN Agency in battle."

"Maybe we can," Denise said. "That's all we can say."

Tom felt the plane's wheels skid as they landed on the ground. He was fully armored once again, shield on. He shook in fear as the plane stopped.

"Tom," Bryan said. "Don't worry about it."

Tom felt stronger now, but not by much, because the plane ground to a halt at that moment. "Let's roll," Gary said.

Tom was the first man off the plane, gun held out. He stopped dead at the bottom of the stairs. Lewis Trenton was waiting for them.

"Good evening, gentlemen," he said. "I've been waiting for you for a while. What took you so long?"

Hatred brimmed in Tom's expression. "Come to do the

dirty deed yourself, eh?"

"What?" Trenton seemed taken aback.

"I know there was a plot to murder me. You almost did it on my way out." Tom seethed with anger. "Now, prepare to be taken in for questioning."

Bryan and Gary were now flanking Tom, ready to fight.

Trenton laughed. "You amuse me…you didn't figure it out?"

Tom realized that Trenton wasn't carrying any weapons in his hands. Tom lowered his carbine slowly. "What is this?" he said.

"I'm Lewis Trenton, supposedly in the inner circle of Frederick of the RED Agency. That's what you think, and that's what Frederick thinks."

Tom was utterly dumbfounded. "What are you talking about?"

"I'm actually Lewis Trenton, BLUE Agency spy."

A surge of realization gripped Tom. "How…how…"

Just then, a BLUE Agency car pulled up. David stepped out of the driver's seat, pistol in hand. Bob exited the back, and behind him Denise. Finally, I stepped out of the shotgun seat.

I saw Tom standing there, and Trenton only a few feet away. I raised my gun.

Trenton laughed. "And just when I got done explaining it the first time!"

I looked at Tom, then back at Trenton. "Listen, I don't know what you're talking about, but you're under arrest."

"You can't do that, Jones," said Trenton.

Tom looked like he was going to say something.

"Because I"—he took out his wallet and displayed a shiny

BLUE symbol—"am a BLUE agent."

My jaw dropped. I realized…the first night when Trenton took out his wallet…it wasn't a bribe. "What? How in the world…but what about…and the negotiations? You were…"

"Please, allow me to explain." Trenton cleared his throat. Everyone else just looked as surprised as me. Except for Denise, who stood straight and still. "First, I would like to apologize. We've had to keep this an absolute secret from everyone, even you, Josiah. No one but Denise has known who I really am.

"The negotiations were a ploy by the GREEN and BLUE Agencies together. No one knew about this but Denise and I, whom she sent to be her spy. This was why I went to talk with Oulaire in private—we were a team all along. He knew that I was a BLUE agent."

I looked toward Denise. This couldn't be true. However, she just nodded. I looked back at Trenton, dumbstruck.

"You're probably wondering why the information that Tom had only told his fellow BLUE agents and Oulaire…well, why that leaked."

"Yes, how did it leak?" Tom said angrily.

"You didn't realize, though I blatantly told Josiah, that there was a RED agent in your midst," Trenton said with a wide smile.

"I thought you meant Tom." I said.

"No, no, no," Trenton said. "Wasn't it obvious? He was always in a hurry…talking to himself, with his hand up to his mouth."

No way.

"It was the waiter!" Trenton said.

"What?"

"Didn't you notice? He was always scratching his face.

He had unusual sleeve buttons. He talked to himself *while* he was scratching his face and no other time. He was a RED spy sent to get information from Tom that he could unwittingly say, and he did in front of Oulaire and the waiter. Thus, the waiter sent the message home that we knew about the RED's plans of attack."

"But then why did Oulaire side with the RED?" Tom said. The traces of anger in his voice were beginning to fade.

Trenton was suddenly solemn. "I should have suspected it all along. When he would talk to me, it was almost contemptuous. And he spent altogether too much time talking to his waiter." His voice sounded graver than I had ever heard it.

"Is…is this true, Denise?" I asked.

"Yes." Denise had the same solemn tone of voice as Trenton.

"So all this time, Trenton has been working for us and we've been hating him." Guilt replaced the fear in my thoughts.

"Don't feel bad about it. This was what I was aiming for, so you made my mission a total success."

I smiled.

"But there really was a plot to murder me," Tom said to himself. "I feel almost honored."

"You will be honored," Denise said.

"Huh?" Tom turned around.

"As soon as we win this battle—and we *will* win—you will be commended to the All-Force 5." Denise smiled.

Tom's jaw dropped. I looked at him with a surprised and excited expression. Tom had been trying to make it into the All-Force 5 for years…I saw him feel his dream come true.

"Now, we have no time for that, do we?" said Tom. "Let's get this started. And folks, be prepared to die. For your country. For the BLUE Agency!"

"Okay...a bit too dramatic there," Denise said. "Tom, Gary, Bryan—you can go with Trenton. Everyone else goes with David.

I laughed. Five minutes ago Tom would have been appalled at the idea of going in a car with Trenton. Now, it looked like there was nothing in the world he'd rather do.

CHAPTER 22: FOR OUR COUNTRY

"I'm glad you're back," Denise said.

"Thank you for the All-Force 5 badge...but I didn't even get the GREEN on our side like I was supposed to."

"That doesn't matter. You're a hero."

"How so?" Tom asked.

"Under a death threat you were still loyal to the BLUE Agency, even after all the stuff you've already been through in your experiences here. You're an example for the entire agency, and for that you deserve what you get. And I heard about what you did in the hangar. Truly, this was what a BLUE agent is meant to do."

"We have no time to talk about this now. We can't have ceremonies this instant," Bryan said. "We need to have everyone guarding every entrance possible. Bar up the doors and make sure no one can get in without the universal password."

"That's my job to say. Let's go, everyone. Bar the doors."

I headed off to my room to find anything I could use to block off a door. There were some extra bedposts under my own bed, and I took those to my assigned entrance.

As I slid the posts between the handles, the loudspeakers said, "Please bar the doors to your assigned entrance. Be constantly prepared for attack. Wear armor and shields at all times, and keep a weapon on your person."

The message repeated itself twice, and by the second time, I had a lurching feeling in my stomach. They were coming, and soon.

The entire agency was once again in a huge hustle, everyone running around and doing errands to help people stay on track and cut off any entrance the agencies might have.

Intensity hung everywhere, and it was audible in everyone's conversation. No one talked for extended periods of time—even conversations with Bob, David, Gary and Tom were stilted. At least, when they were one-on-one conversations. When we were all together, talk was about the upcoming battle and strategies for getting the RED agents out.

"I like the hit-and-run tactics," Tom said. "They've always worked well in smaller groups, or even picking off the front lines in larger ones. Get three down, move to the back. They have no time to hit you."

"I like just barreling through the entire line, shooting as I go," I said. "That helps to push people out of the base, and I've found it effective."

"But everyone's shooting the heck out of you," Gary said. "I like moving as I shoot, shooting one, then moving over. It works every time."

"Snipe from somewhere high if you can find one, or just pick people off from behind something," Bob said. "Of course, you always have to have someone watching your back or you'll just get pistol whipped. The shield doesn't take that very well, especially if they hit it right on the generator."

"What? You seriously can't get pistol whipped without the shield—"

I broke off. A siren blared from overhead.

They were coming.

I jumped up and slipped my head into my helmet, running to my assigned entrance with Bob and Gary, behind a barricade of desks and Plywood boarded to the door, which was barred with bedposts and metal poles.

Everyone was silently crouching at his entrance. It was a stomach-churning experience. We sat—waited—no sign that there was anyone alive except in our peripheral vision.

"This is creepy," Bob said, who was on my channel.

A felt hot—almost like a fever. Then a rush of cold set me shivering. I realized it was the coolant in the fabric to cool down my body. Then it came.

Boom. A low sound with a small explosion. Missiles.

Boom.

Boom.

It was coming from our door.

Then it came from somewhere else.

Boom.

Boom.

Bang!

Boom!

CRACK! The Plexiglas broke behind the boards that our group had secured into the door.

The plywood split over the door in front of us. The bed-posts bent and flew off the door handles. Suddenly, a surge of RED agents had broken the doors off. A bedpost flew toward us. I caught it and whipped it around, slamming a RED agent. Unfortunately, he wasn't out, so I sealed it with a low-level blast.

More and more RED agents pushed past the desks. I stood and ran backward, firing at the agents to the unarmored pieces.

"Where did they get all these people?" I shouted over the helmet percoms and the din, the roar of the soldiers pounding their feet against the metal floor.

"I don't know," Gary said, "but they definitely have more than we thought!"

I heard more cracking and the sound of more agents rush-ing in. The sound of stun carbines became ubiquitous, unceas-ing. I started to apply some of the strategies we had talked about.

I stood atop a desk and began to snipe down agents, un-til several RED fired simultaneously. My gun began to over-charge, so I leapt from the top of the desk, holding the trigger and firing aimlessly in the air to release the excess.

I pushed through the crowd mercilessly, firing at the plac-es I knew would render them unconscious. I felt crushed by RED agents shooting at me. I jumped-kicked one down, and caused a domino effect clearing the path through the huge crowds of RED agents ready to attack.

Agents ran throughout the building, scattering them-selves to get every possible person down. *We're never going to get all these people,* I thought. *Half of them must be GREEN agents in RED guise.* Anger pumped throughout my brain, in my blood. I could feel the dislike for Jean Claude De Oulaire and his regime. *He's the enemy now. He's a RED agent like the rest of them.*

I kept firing, but many of the people at whom I was firing dodged and fired back. Everyone was scattered...there was hardly anyone left in the lobby. I wondered....

Another surge of people flooded the room. We were overwhelmed by hundreds of RED agents overtaking the area. I was left there, standing and terrified among the crowd. BLUE agents were now going down because they couldn't transfer their energy anywhere else, causing their shields or guns to overload. RED agents still fell, but now they were a thick pack. *If only I could go on the edge of overload, then do one of David's shield-bomb things.*

I could hardly see the other BLUE agents—but I didn't care. This is my time to fight, vengeance for the things they had done to other people. Murder. Cruelty. Crime.

I expertly jumped and fired at the RED agents in my way to get through to the other BLUE agents. I had to run to get to the line of agents that was slowly trying to pick off the RED lines.

I joined in the curve of people standing together. We were fighting and almost certainly dying for our country.

"Josiah!" I heard a yell in my percom. It was Tom, calling me over to the other end of the line. I did a duck-run-and-fire along the ground, hitting between the armor plates in the leg to knock down people in the front line as I ran across. I could immediately see Tom's problem.

He was crouching in the back behind the line, pressing the buttons on his shield. They flickered on and off, words on the screen telling him about a programming error.

"This is not good," I said. "How are we going to fix this?"

"I don't know!" he yelled.

Suddenly, my shield flickered and died, showing the same error. Tom and I ran backward along with other agents, shooting to pick off anyone we could without hitting one of our own.

"It looks like the RED have planted a bug in the shields system. We don't have time to reprogram it," I said. I saw several other agents' shields go down

"But there *is* a reprogramming button on here," Tom said.

"I'll try to remember from doing the shield generators."

"By the way, how did they get past that?"

"We intercepted your personal communications," said a voice I knew all too well. He was speaking into my percom's channel.

"This can't be good," I said to myself.

"Don't worry. It isn't." The voice of Frederick broke into a sinister laugh.

CHAPTER 23: FOR OUR AGENCY

"I don't care what you say, Frederick," I said to him.

"That's exactly your problem—you don't care what I say. Remember what I said about Tom? The part where my right-hand-man was going to kill him?" Frederick's voice sounded more evil than I had ever heard it sound before.

"Yes, your right hand man. He's not anymore, is he? Cut all illegitimate contacts, computer."

"Access denied," said the computer. It almost sounded evil at this point.

"Frederick!"

"Yes, Mr. Jones?"

I hated to have my perfectly good name spoiled by this man.

"Do you know why I am a member of the RED Agency?" said Frederick, not waiting for a reply.

"Why?" I struggled to reprogram Tom's shield. The display flickered and flashed with hesitation.

"Because I am one who does want to be taken seriously, and when I was attempting to join the BLUE Agency at age nineteen, no one there took me seriously. And do you know what happened when I became leader of the RED Agency?"

I didn't say a word. I was reprogramming Tom's shield. *Almost done,* I thought.

"Everyone in this BLUE Agency takes me very, very seriously. Do you get that? Everyone respects me. No one fools around with Fred. Although that is not a name that would usually instill fear, I have turned it into an ultimate weapon. And do you know what I think?"

Almost done…

"I think you're my next victim."

This time the voice came from right behind me and in my percom. I looked up, and the towering figure of Frederick was behind me. His hulking frame was standing far above me, and even though I'm tall for my age, I could never say that I was as tall as Frederick Heschmann.

Done. I stood up after finishing the programming. I blocked the pistol whip with my carbonyssium carbine. I was once again locked into battle with Fred, the evil leader of the RED Agency.

"Go!" I yelled as Tom's shield bubbled into existence.

I pulled back and fired three shots at Frederick, but they simply ricocheted back at me and were absorbed by my armor. "You can't simply shoot me down," said Frederick. He took his shot. I glanced the fire off with the side of my own bulletproof gun.

"Not fair," he said.

"Who ever said this game was fair?"

I jumped and shot at where I thought his shield generator was, only to be disappointed that it wasn't the correct location. "Who said it was fair that the GREEN Agency was on your side? Who said it was fair that you keep trying to kill us?"

"No one did but me," said Frederick. "You're right. It isn't fair. That's why I'll win this battle."

"Not while I still have breath in my body!" Anger surged. I felt the blood pumping behind my ears, and then my body cooling as the coolant liquid pulsed over me. Frederick only laughed and stepped back. This made me angrier. Blood pumped faster. Heart beat hard. I felt it thumping in my chest. Everything turned off...my stomach stopped digesting, and all the other normal activities in my body ceased, giving me energy in one place. My arms felt anxious, ready to disable the shield and take down Frederick.

"This one's for my country!" I yelled, as I slammed my carbonyssium carbine against his arm. It bounced off the shield, but a zapping sound emanated.

I was draining the energy.

Frederick, in anger, fired three shots that only went back into the air via my energy transfer.

"For my family!" I hacked again against his arm. The shield weakened.

A loud sound rolled through the entire building, like a stampede of animals coming to attack. I looked around. It was probably the GREEN Agency coming to seal the deal. We were done for. I closed my eyes, pulling forward, poising myself to go down swinging

It was the GREEN Agency. There were scores of men rushing in through all the broken entrances. Everyone stopped for a second, and then came a rousing shout from Jean Claude de Oulaire: "For the BLUE Agency!"

What? For the BLUE Agency? How...but...I thought...

And there was Oulaire, standing right in the front line, ready for any action that was to come his way. He was shouting a battle cry.

Frederick was caught off guard, and his arm was there for the asking.

This gave me my final chance. I slammed my carbine against Frederick's arm; his shield was disabled from the impact. He fell to the floor. "Ha! Ha! You can't..."

"No!"

Lewis Trenton's BLUE-uniformed frame leaped from the crowd, flying through the high-ceilinged lobby, leg outstretched, ready to kick Frederick down, and his gun brandished and ready to fire.

I saw the realization, the knowledge of the double-cross zoom across Frederick's face in that moment. I saw the realization turn to anger. Frederick clutched Lewis shin and twisted his body, throwing him to the ground.

Frederick flicked a pistol into his right hand and slammed it against my chest, head, and arm. The carbine I had held fell out of my hands. In an act of bravery, Lewis stood up. "No!" he shouted.

The pistol knocked out my shield. It would never come back again. Frederick turned, aimed his pistol, and fired right between the chest and abdomen plates of Lewis' armor.

I saw Lewis' eyes widen behind his helmet as he fell backward, clutching his stomach. Before I could give my horrified reaction, Frederick spun on a dime, pistol aimed, ready to fire.

I tried to reach for my gun. It was too far away. Frederick squeezed the trigger.

I felt pain in my stomach. The world blurred. I fell back, back through what felt like Infinity. I felt nothing but the pain I had just sensed.

So there I was left lying beside Lewis. I turned my head to look at him. He looked straight back at me, and nodded.

With a roar of pain and anger, he stood to fight again, firing blast after blast at the RED agents around him. He was fighting on.

Frederick looked over at him with surprise and anger that I could see through his helmet.

Reactively, with great agility that sprang from excitement and adrenaline, I locked both hands around my carbine and jumped off my back into the air from strength I didn't know I had.

Frederick turned to face me.

I aimed the carbine between the armor plates…Frederick was on his way to prison…no more killings…no crime from the RED….

"Good night," I said with surprising strength. And with one squeeze of the trigger, Frederick was out like a light.

Tom, who had watched the entire thing from his battle stance, cheered. "Way to go, Josiah! That's why you're the top agent."

"But how are these GREEN agents for us now?" I said feebly. "Didn't they say that they were for the RED Agency?"

I looked around the lobby. There were very few RED agents left. The lobby was still crowded, however, because of the surge of GREEN agents that had entered. Oulaire was standing in the center of it all, firing like mad, and avoiding shots with insane barrel rolls and jumps.

It was only seconds later that Oulaire said, "Drop. Your. Weapons." He emphasized each word for effect.

He looked now at Frederick, who was leaning against a wall. He looked almost comatose.

"And this man," he said, "whom I have no idea how he escaped from prison, is to be put in high-security. You will never see Frederick Heschmann again."

A loud cheer erupted from the BLUE Agency. I couldn't believe it. We owed it all to the GREEN Agency—the ones we had thought were against us. We had finally triumphed for the last time.

CHAPTER 24: FINAL SCORE

"Josiah, what were you thinking?"

I had just relayed the story of how Lewis and I had both fought after being shot by Frederick. Lewis and I were leaning against the wall in the lobby. Much of the pain in my stomach had dissipated, and most of the RED agents were now barely awake and without weapons.

"He was a hero," said Lewis. Denise looked at him with gratitude.

"Here...let me see what Frederick did..." Denise pulled back the torn fabric on my armor. Only a small, scarred wound was left. "You're lucky he didn't take off more skin. Obviously he wasn't trying to kill you; otherwise he would have used a more powerful weapon or weapon mode."

"But then why did he shoot me, if not to kill?" I asked.

"I...I don't have an answer for that. Maybe he wanted to

keep you for questioning or ransom, but that's something we may never find out."

Three days later. All of the RED agents who were at the invasion of the BLUE base were charged for their crimes.

Me? I stuck around at the BLUE Agency base. My wounds were fairly well healed—I could do everything a normal secret agent could do.

I sat in Denise's office, which held David, Denise, Tom, Gary, Bob, Lewis, and I, plus the special guest appearance of none other than Jean Claude de Oulaire.

I shook the tall general's hand. "I'd like to thank you so much for saving the BLUE Agency. We were really done for without you."

"I'm glad that I could be of help," Jean Claude said. He smiled widely. "It was really you and Trenton who stopped Frederick, even in the face of death."

I smiled back. No need to mention that I couldn't have died from his blast. "But...I have a question. You were in with the BLUE Agency the entire time? Or am I mistaken?"

"You're correct," Jean Claude said. "We simply ordered for our men to go to the RED Agency headquarters. That doesn't mean that we were on their side."

"Then why did you send the men to the RED base, then?"

"You don't trust us? It was because we were invading their base! We wanted the RED to assume that we were on their side, when actually we took over the entire base and caught them off guard." He laughed. "You must not trust in first impressions. Don't worry—that building is now property of the BLUE Agency."

"Really?"

The others, who were chatting behind me, laughed at a joke Bob had told.

"Agent D is filing the deed to it right now. So, you can use that as your backup facility. The only problem is, if the RED Agency ever regains power, they'll know where you are."

I laughed. "That won't be a problem. They're not going anywhere."

Jean Claude's face straightened. "I would not be so sure about that," he said. "You must keep your guard up, BLUE Agency. I don't want to see you go down in flames. Oh! And you are probably wondering why I wanted to cover up my true colors if Mr. Trenton was not even for the RED?"

"It was the waiter, wasn't it?" I asked.

Jean Claude smiled slyly. "After Trenton left, I told my waiter to have a word with me. Accused him, proved him guilty, and confiscated his microphones in his sleeves. I got out of him when they were to attack and turned him over to the authorities."

I snickered. "Good job, General."

"No problem. Now if you will excuse me, there are matters I must take care of back in Paris. I hope you understand."

"All right. Thank you so much," I said.

"It is my pleasure to work with you." He looked at his silver watch, which was glinting in the sun. "Goodbye."

Without another word, the general silently walked out of the room taking huge strides and ducking as to avoid hitting his head on the relatively short doorway.

"Denise, I didn't see you or KC during the battle. Where were you?" I asked, standing to join the rest of our party.

"I was fighting with KC in a hall. Actually, where is KC

right now? She needs some congratulations."

"I'll get her on her percom."

I dialed the number. "Hey, Josiah…if you're wondering where I am, I'm on my way."

"Okay," I said. "You already knew we were here?"

"I passed Oulaire in the hallway, and he told me you were in Denise's office. Why didn't you guys tell me you were meeting there?"

"It's not a very serious meeting." As I said that, everyone laughed at another joke from Bob.

"Okay," KC said. "Well you still should have told me."

I rolled my eyes. "Over and out, KC."

It was two weeks later that I was in Denise's Seclab with David and Denise.

"Have you visited Frederick in prison, yet?" I asked.

"They don't let him have visitors. He's pretty well locked up, which is probably a good thing. I'm very glad, personally." Denise leaned back and popped a small handful of popcorn into her mouth.

"I think that we could have done better in locking him up. I mean, high security prison is obviously high security, but we could have something a bit more. He already escaped from a solitary-confinement cell that had barely fewer guards, and now they expect him to stay put in this one."

"I don't think we have to worry about that…" I said. "At least, for now."

I sighed and stood up slowly, stretched, and took long, slow steps across the white-carpeted and clean floor to the tall silver refrigerator-freezer. I pulled the door open and looked for the right drink, selecting, thinking. I pulled a green one off the shelf, trying to honor Oulaire's nobility in saving the entire BLUE Agency, and the entire world. The RED Agency was very close this time to winning, and I was forever grateful for the services of the GREEN Agency. Even if they had to cover it with a façade.

I sat down once again on the couch, in the soft seat next to David and across from Denise, who was sitting in a big beanbag chair.

"So, what did you think about that last act of the battle?" I said. "I totally wasn't expecting the GREEN Agency to begin attacking the RED. That was the most unexpected thing in the entire battle."

"I say that I could have anticipated it if I were more deeply involved in the negotiations," David said. "I don't think I would have been surprised. But being unprepared as I was, I definitely didn't expect that to happen. Although Denise had been suspicious looking."

"I had no idea. Both Tom and Lewis confirmed it, so… anyway. Did you hear about the building?"

"No," David said.

"Let me tell him!" I said. "We have the deed to it. The GREEN Agency invaded it and they're giving the deed over to the BLUE Agency. In a few months, we'll have the entire thing ready as a backup for this building. And we can rent the outside room as an office space."

""Or we could possibly house a secondary New York regiment," David said. "That could be a possibility."

The room was quiet for a few minutes. I had forgotten about my drink. I popped open the tab and took a draw. Tasted like good old green. I still felt the satisfaction and gratitude for the GREEN Agency sweeping over me as I took long draws.

"David," Denise said in a more serious tone, "we were thinking of going on summer break to Ohio and coming over to your house. It's near Cleveland, right?"

"Right," he said. "We live a few miles away from the city, sort of in a suburb."

"I think we can handle that." I smiled. Everything was turning out well.

It had been so flurried at the BLUE Agency that we had forgotten about my birthday. My fourteenth birthday. So, a month after the battle, we celebrated my belated birthday party (it had been three weeks previous that I had actually turned fourteen).

The Seclab held Denise, David, Bob, Tom, KC, Lewis, Gary, and me. We had this time Greek food—one of my new favorites since I moved to the BLUE Agency for a year. We dressed in dress suits on my request. I just liked the feel of being a true agent for my birthday.

Several presents were stacked against the wall. *I wonder if I'll actually be able to take them home. We're only almost done with our year here—it's gone so fast, with all that's been going on. It's something to think about.*

"Happy birthday," Denise said. "And thanks for inviting us. This is great food."

The walls had changed colors to look like windows outside. Steve had even expanded the star application for me so we could change the walls to reflect different environments. Currently we were looking out on the city of New York as we sat at a table with a tabletop of glass.

I cut my knife into a chicken kebab. "I'm glad you could all come."

The evening filled me with a great feeling—the feeling that my friends were around me and that they were happy to be in my life. I felt at home.

The following days flew by like they didn't exist. There were days of stress, days of leisure, and nights where I would look up and know that I would miss the BLUE Agency.

CHAPTER 25: DAVID

It was a cool summer night when we sneaked out of the house.

"Are you sure that map is accurate?" Denise, who generally didn't trust anything from the Internet, definitely didn't feel secure with a map from it.

"Don't worry about it," I said. I felt relaxed, even though I had anticipation running pure through my body. It was beginning to feel chilly this evening in mid-June. If David were wearing summer clothes, he would be shivering right now. "Do we have the flashlight?" I asked.

Denise wordlessly tossed the flashlight to me. I clicked it on, illuminating the map in small circles of light.

"So we walk for about a mile west, then a sixteenth of a mile north, and we'll be right there. Shouldn't be too long. We take Jay Avenue." I began to walk, sockless feet in my shoes.

It felt weird, having spent only a year in school and yet

more than a year growing up. My age was slowly beginning to match up with my age in the imaginary world. It felt weird. And it also was odd to celebrate my birthday months before the real thing.

It was also weird, having Denise, KC, and myself a year younger when we came back. I was shorter, less muscular, generally smaller.

A night breeze swept over the streets. I shivered in my jeans and shirt I had hastily thrown on once everyone had gone to bed.

"What does it feel like?" I asked. "Finally meeting your brother in real life?"

I could see behind the normal snappish, clipping Denise a feeling of true emotion and excitement at seeing her brother again for real, for the first time of her life.

"I...I don't know what to think." I saw a tear begin to form in her eye, but her voice was not at all choked. "I mean... we should have grown up together, known each other better than boss-to-employee. We're twins."

"I know. But you can know him as your brother from now on. And you know him in two worlds." I swallowed. "Not a lot of separated twins get that."

Denise nodded. "I know," she said. The tear in her eye dripped down her cheek, but her voice was still unwavering. "I can't wait to talk to him. You know, in the real world."

The rest of the mile-and-a-sixteenth-long walk was very short, breezy, and wordless. I held up the flashlight and the map, looking at house after house to match the numbers. After three blocks of the wrong numbers, I knew which one was it.

Above the door hung a lantern, and beside the lantern was a porch swing on which David sat eating a bowl of ice cream. Another bowl was sitting next to him.

He saw us coming and set down his bowl. I looked at him. It seemed so odd to see him in casual clothes. I was so used to black leather jackets, BLUE shirts, and dark jeans. But now, he was standing with a broad smile on his face, eyes bare, and walking across his porch.

Denise left my side and ran as fast as she could, leaping all three steps onto the porch. She wrapped her arms around her brother, and tears flowed freely down her face.

And for the first time ever, I saw a tear coming from the right eye of David as he embraced his sister. "I saved a bowl of ice cream for you. It's still cold if you want some."

David looked at me and nodded. I smiled back.

I turned around and looked up at the stars.

I was happy to be alive.

THE END

ACKNOWLEDGMENTS

Once again, I find myself writing the acknowledgments with far too many people to acknowledge. Well, to start out, I have my family, who have always helped me through the tough days.

Second, my friends. I love you all. You've been loyal fans and great people to tell me that I'm annoying the heck out of you always talking about books.

Once again to Chris Baty and the participants of National Novel Writing Moth. Your unending help and inspiration has made me push through to now have written six novels, two of them published, by age fifteen. (It's still amazing to me.)

I've got a big round of writing and editing inspiration for this one. First, Elmore Hammes, for being my second set of eyes for the plot. Faith Ann Carroll, my always diligent editor, thanks for all the work you've done as well as the compliments and encouragements along the way.

And this time, I've added a couple more authors to my thank-you list. First and foremost, the one who definitely has inspired me the most, Christopher Paolini. Probably one of the most amazing people of all time. J.K. Rowling is a new favorite of mine. Thanks, J.K., for giving me such great companionship in Harry, Ron, and Hermione throughout this summer. I hope you're actually able to read this, which would mean that you're reading my book (I would be honored!).

For the publishing, I have to give a huge thank you for Stacey Cochran, not only for being a big supporter of Double Life, but also assisting me with all the publishing stuff an author like me needs to know. Jeremy Robinson, once again, Elmore again, and my friend Clint Kellams, for believing in my idea enough to help me jump-start in publishing.

I find myself once again running out of paper, so if you feel like you should have been acknowledged, I'm sorry I couldn't get you on these pages. If you had any influence on this book at all, I appreciate you infinitely.

Sincerely,

Dawson Vosburg

ABOUT THE AUTHOR

DAWSON VOSBURG was born in 1994 in Anderson, Indiana, where he still attends high school at Liberty Christian. He's currently working on the third and final installment in the Adventures of Josiah Jones. His hobbies include art, fillmaking, and guitar.

www.ingramcontent.com/pod-product-compliance
Lightning Source LLC
Chambersburg PA
CBHW031325170626
46807CB00002B/582